# HORROR HIGH

## IT'S THE STUFF OF NIGHTMARES

## DEADLY RUMOURS

I shielded my eyes from the sun.

And then I saw him. A teenage boy. Wearing jeans and a yellow T-shirt. He was standing over the falls. Right on the edge.

I gasped . . . I hadn't expected him to be standing there.

He didn't see me. He was staring straight down, down to the jagged black rocks below the falling water.

He took a step forward.

My heart stopped.

I realized what he was about to do.

"Stop!" I screamed. "Don't jump! Please . . . don't jump!"

R. L. STINE

# HORROR HIGH

## DeAdly RuMOuRs

SCHOLASTIC

Scholastic Children's Books
An imprint of Scholastic Ltd
Euston House, 24 Eversholt Street
London, NW1 1DB, UK
Registered office: Westfield Road, Southam, Warwickshire, CV47 0RA
SCHOLASTIC and associated logos are trademarks and
or registered trademarks of Scholastic Inc.

First published in the US as *The Dead Girlfriend* by Scholastic Inc, 1993
First published in the UK by Scholastic Publications Ltd, 1994
This edition published in the UK by Scholastic Ltd, 2009

Text copyright © Robert L. Stine, 1993

ISBN 978 1407 11152 0

British Library Cataloguing-in-Publication Data
A CIP catalogue record for this book is available
from the British Library

The right of Robert L. Stine to be identified as the author of this work
has been asserted by him.

Printed in the UK by CPI Bookmarque, Croydon, CR0 4TD
Papers used by Scholastic Children's Books are made from wood grown in
sustainable forests.

1 3 5 7 9 10 8 6 4 2

www.scholastic.co.uk/zone

# One

The first time I saw Louis Morgan, he terrified me.

I probably should have known then – at that very first moment, staring into the sun at him from my bike – to stay away.

Danger here.

Danger and fear.

I think I knew at that moment that Louis meant trouble. But a person doesn't always listen to these signals. A person doesn't always listen to her sensible self. At least, I didn't.

And before I knew it, I found myself trapped by Louis.

Caught up in his sadness. Caught up in his mystery.

A mystery that began in murder.

It all started on such a beautiful day, warm and promising, fresh as only a day in late April can be.

I borrowed my brother Jake's bike and went riding. I wanted to explore Shocklin Falls, our new home.

Jake's bike was a clunky BMX, heavy and slow, and the seat was too high for me. (Do you *believe* I'm shorter than my little brother? It's so annoying.) But my 21-speed had been stolen just before we moved. So what choice did I have?

I'm seventeen and I have my driver's licence. But you can't really explore in a car.

Bike riding is my passion. I love the rush of wind against my face, the feel of the pedals under my trainers, the control, the way it makes my legs throb and my heart pound.

The total *freedom* of it.

You can't feel that in a car.

Dad promised I could buy a new bike as soon as the insurance company paid for the stolen one. I really didn't want to wait that long. But Dad wasn't in any mood for arguments.

He and Mum are still unpacking boxes. I think they'll be unpacking boxes until next Christmas! You just don't realize how much *stuff* a family of four owns until you move to a new town.

Anyway, I took off on Jake's bike. I'm such a shrimp. I should've lowered the seat. But I was too impatient to get away and explore.

I was wearing shorts and a bright blue sleeveless T-shirt. It was the first really warm spring day, and the afternoon sun felt hot on my back.

I had just washed my hair, which is long and blonde and very straight. I had tied it up. I knew the sun would dry it.

The air smelled so sweet! All down my street, the dogwood trees had blossomed. It was like riding under majestic white arches, so pretty and unreal.

Prettier than real life, I thought.

I get these kinds of thoughts when I'm out bike riding.

It didn't take too long to explore Shocklin Falls. It's a very small town, a suburb of Glenview. The college where Mum and Dad are going to start teaching next term is at one end. Then come quiet streets, shady under rows of old trees, lined with small, nice-looking houses.

The big, expensive houses are out by the falls on the other side of town. And in the middle is a small shopping district – two-storey buildings, mostly, a two-screen cinema, a bank, and a post office. Not much else. The nearest mall is in Glenview.

I rode slowly past the small shops. For a Saturday afternoon, the town wasn't very crowded. I think most people were at home doing spring-cleaning or gardening.

An old car rumbled past, filled with teenagers, its windows open, radio blaring. The noise drew frowns and headshakes from two elderly women about to cross Main Street arm in arm.

A bike shop on the corner caught my eye. I climbed off

Jake's bike and walked it up to the front window. I pressed my nose against the glass, peering inside. It looked like a pretty good selection. I'd definitely have to check it out later.

I climbed back onto Jake's bike and coasted unsteadily off the curb back onto the street. Is that all there is to town? I wondered.

Yep. I'd seen it all.

I circled round once again, then headed towards the falls.

I hadn't seen the famous falls yet. Mrs Pratte, the estate agent who sold us our house, couldn't stop raving about how beautiful and spectacular they are.

So I was saving the best part of my tour for last.

Mrs Pratte described the falls as rising up high on a sheer rock-cliff, then cascading straight down like a steamy, white curtain into the wide river below.

She was good at describing things, which I guess you need to be if you're going to sell property. Anyway, she said it was as pretty as Niagara Falls, except much smaller, of course, and you could see three towns from up at the top.

I followed Main Street past the shopping district and soon found myself in the fancy part of Shocklin Falls. Big houses. Some of them looked like *mansions* to me! A lot of them had teams of gardeners working, planting beds of flowers and weeding and clearing away the dead leaves.

I had a little scare when a snarling German shepherd

came bounding after me. Its owner was yelling for the dog to come back, but of course the dog paid no attention.

I began pedalling furiously, standing up to get better speed. Luckily, the dog gave up halfway down the street and contented itself to end the chase and bark out a warning for me to stay away.

"OK, OK. I can take a hint!" I called back to it, still pedalling standing up.

The big houses gave way to woods. The trees were still mostly bare, the spring leaves just beginning to open. A squirrel scampered up a tree, startled by my silent, gliding intrusion.

I found the cycle path Mrs Pratte had described. It curved through the woods, climbing higher as it went, becoming steeper and steeper as it made its way up through the thick trees.

After about a ten-minute ride, I found myself at the top. I was pleased to see that I wasn't at all out of breath. Being in good shape is really important to me. It's one reason I always prefer my bike to a car.

I kept pedalling. The woods were all to my right now. To my left – the steep cliff-edge, a sheer drop to black rocks below.

I slowed down. There was no fence or anything. At some

points, the cycle path came within a half a metre of the cliff-edge. And the path was really curvy.

I heard the falls before I saw them. A soft, steady roar that grew louder as I approached.

And then the path curved, and the falls were right in front of me.

How can I describe them? They were dazzling.

The white water fell straight down, sparkling like a million diamonds, splashing back up in a shimmery white mist.

Looking down, I could see the wide brown river flowing between green banks. And I could see far into the distance, over trees, over fields. I could see the town, tiny like it was miniature, and beyond it another town, and then, in the misty distance, a third town.

I slowed to a stop. The cycle path ended abruptly at a tall pile of grey granite rocks.

I shielded my eyes from the sun.

And then I saw him.

A teenage boy. Wearing jeans and a yellow T-shirt. He was standing over the falls. Right on the edge.

I gasped and gripped the handlebars. I hadn't expected anyone to be standing there.

He didn't see me. He was staring straight down, down to the jagged black rocks below the falling water.

Still staring straight down, he took a step forward.

My heart stopped.

I realized what he was about to do.

"Stop!" I screamed, trying to be heard over the roar of the falls. "Don't jump! Please – don't jump!"

# Two

He cried out and stepped back.

My screams had startled him.

I jumped off the bike and hurried towards him. The bike clattered onto the rocks behind me.

"Hey!" he called. His expression changed from surprise to confusion. He jammed his hands into his jeans pockets and he moved away from the edge, towards me.

He was tall and very good-looking. He was really tanned. He had a cleft chin. He stared at me with striking green eyes.

I guess I was staring hard at him. That's how I managed to see his face so clearly.

"I thought you were someone else," he said, shouting over the sound of the falls. He smiled. A crooked smile, but very gorgeous.

I think I fell in love with him then. Or something like

that. I'm not sure. It's impossible to explain. I was so embarrassed about shouting like that.

"I thought you were going to. . ." I started, but I didn't want to finish my sentence.

He was still smiling, hands jammed into his pockets, his yellow T-shirt fluttering in the wind. "You what?"

"I'm sorry," I stammered. "I saw you at the edge, and. . ."

I get a slight stammer whenever I'm really nervous. And believe me, I was really stammering now!

He laughed. He had a great laugh. Sort of tossed his head back and crinkled those incredible green eyes.

"You thought I was going to jump?" The smile faded. His eyes burned into mine, studying me.

I nodded. I could feel my face turn red.

I tugged at my hair. It was still wet.

"I'm just waiting for someone," he said. "Looks like they're not coming."

"I – I've never been up here before," I stammered, lowering my eyes. I didn't like standing there. I don't normally have trouble with heights. But we were so high up, and the drop was so straight, so steep, and the rocks below looked so sharp and pointed.

"D'you go to Glenview High?" he asked.

I shook my head. "Starting on Monday. We've just moved here. From Ohio. I'm Abbie Kiernan," I said awkwardly. I always find it so hard to introduce myself like that. I don't know why.

"Louis Morgan," he said. He removed his hands from his jeans pockets and shook my hand. Very formal.

He grinned.

I loved the cleft in his chin. And I loved the way the wind blew through his hair but it stayed standing up, every hair in place.

I should have seen the sadness in those green eyes.

I should have seen the fear. The dread.

But of course I didn't.

I should have asked him why he was standing right on the cliff-edge like that, staring down so intently into the crashing waters.

But of course I didn't.

Instead, I said, "It's so awesome up here." Pretty lame, but at least I had stopped stammering.

"Yeah," he replied, scratching his chin.

"The town is so ordinary," I went on. "I mean, it's OK. But it's nothing special. You don't expect to find something like this." I motioned to the falls.

Louis's eyes were on the woods behind me. "I . . . uh . . . left my bike back there," he said. "Wait right here. I'll go and get it."

"D'you like to bike ride?" I asked as he headed past me.

"Yeah. A lot," he called back without stopping. He disappeared behind the wide pile of granite rocks.

I wrapped my arms round my chest and stared out at the town below. Even with the afternoon sun high above, it was a little chilly up here.

What a fabulous spot, I thought.

I knew I'd be riding my bike up here often.

I suddenly wondered if I'd be riding it beside Louis. I had this silly idea that we were fated to meet up here. Like an old black-and-white romantic film.

Maybe I'll ask him to go riding next weekend or something, I thought.

I saw him approaching, walking a sleek black racing bike.

No. He must have a girlfriend, I realized, a sinking feeling in my stomach.

He's too good-looking not to have a girlfriend.

He said he was meeting someone up here.

He leaned his bike against one of the big stones and made his way towards me, taking long, slow strides. "So you've just moved here?" he asked, pulling a long strand of grass from my hair.

"Yeah. My parents are going to teach at the college."

"Weird time to move," he said, staring over my shoulder at the falls.

"Tell me about it," I groaned. "Changing schools and everything. It's horrible!"

11

He gazed at me thoughtfully. "Are you a senior?"

"Junior," I replied.

"Have you met anybody? Kids, I mean."

"Just you," I said, laughing.

He laughed, too. A silent laugh that sounded more like coughing.

"Then I guess I should show you around or something," he said, suddenly shy.

He should be on TV, I thought. He's so great-looking!

"I could give you a bike tour of Shocklin Falls," he offered, motioning to his bike. "That'll take a minute or two," he joked.

"Well, I've sort of had the bike tour," I said.

And instantly regretted it.

Why did I say that? I scolded myself. He was offering to ride around with me, and I told him no.

What an idiot I am!

I could feel my face redden again.

Louis stared at me thoughtfully. "I'll introduce you to some Shocklin kids," he said.

"Great!" I gushed. "I mean . . ."

He turned his gaze towards the woods, as if he saw something. "I have this friend," he started. "He's my best buddy. I mean, he's a total dork, but he's my best buddy. Actually, he's a wild man. You'll like him."

"Great," I repeated, starting to stammer again. Was he planning to fix me up with this wild-man friend?

"His name is Jacob," Louis continued, still staring towards the woods. "Jacob Dorsey." He sniggered, as if remembering something funny about Jacob.

"Jacob's parents have to work every Friday night," Louis continued. "So we all get together at Jacob's and have like a party. You know. Every Friday. It's great. It gets pretty wild sometimes."

"Sounds great," I said.

Why couldn't I think of some other word? I scolded myself. How many times in one conversation can a person use the word *great*?

He must think I'm a real dork.

"So would you like to go with me on Friday night? To Jacob's, I mean?" His green eyes seemed to light up as he stared at me expectantly.

"You mean, like a date?" I asked.

*Abbie – get it together!* I ordered myself. *It's not like you've never been on a date before. You were pretty popular back in Middletown.*

"Yeah," Louis said, grinning. "Like a date."

"Sure," I said. "Great!"

*Great?*

Did I really say it again?

13

"Great," he repeated softly. He kicked at the grass with his trainer and glanced at the falls. "I've got to go."

"Me, too," I said.

The sun dipped behind a wide white cloud. The air grew chillier. Shadows slid along the ground.

We made our way across the grass to get our bikes.

I was feeling really good.

It was only my third day in Shocklin Falls. And the first boy I'd met, a really great-looking guy, had asked me out.

Not a bad start, I thought.

Not bad at all.

Louis picked up his bike by the handlebars and walked it over to me. Then we headed round to the other side of the big rocks where I had left mine.

To my surprise, the bike was standing up, tilted against a rock.

I remembered just letting it fall when I went running over to Louis, thinking he was going to jump.

Strange, I thought.

And then I gasped loudly. "Whoa!"

I hurried over to the bike and bent low to examine it.

"Hey – what's going on?" I cried, my heart pounding in my chest.

Both tyres had been slashed to ribbons.

# Three

"I don't believe this," I muttered.

I ran one hand over the cut tyre. A chunk of rubber fell off in my hand.

"Who. . ." I started, but the words caught in my throat.

I was crouched down, staring in total disbelief at the slashed tyres on Jake's bike. Louis was standing right behind me, his shadow falling over me.

"I don't get it," he said quietly. "There's no one else up here."

I gazed up at him. His eyes were narrowed on the woods, as if searching for someone there. I followed his glance. The trees were mostly bare. It would be easy to see someone running away.

The woods were empty.

I shuddered. I suddenly felt cold all over.

"Jake's going to kill me," I whispered, climbing to my feet.

"Who's Jake?" Louis asked, still searching the woods.

"My little brother. It's his bike."

Louis scowled. "I'll help you walk it home," he said glumly, avoiding my eyes.

"That's OK," I said. "I can—"

"No." He grabbed the handlebars of Jake's bike. "Take my bike. I'll walk this one," he snapped. He suddenly sounded very angry.

I obediently took his bike. We began to walk side by side along the bike path.

"This is so stupid," I said. "Why would someone do this to me?"

Louis didn't answer.

"I mean, who would climb all the way up to the top of the falls just to wreck some stranger's bike?" I continued, my voice trembling.

Louis still didn't reply.

His angry expression startled me into silence.

Why was *he* so angry? It wasn't *his* bike!

His mood had changed so quickly, it frightened me.

We followed the path as it curved down through the woods. The sun remained behind the clouds. The woods were shadowy now, shadowy and cold. As if spring had left and winter had returned.

It seemed to take forever to get down to the street.

I felt so awkward. I wanted to talk, to say something. Anything. But Louis kept his eyes lowered to the ground, his jaw clenched. I could see the veins throbbing angrily at his temples.

So I remained silent, too.

I just didn't get it. He volunteered to walk me home, after all. I wasn't *forcing* him.

Was he angry with me?

I was totally confused. It didn't make any sense.

The ground levelled out when we reached Main Street. The sun reappeared, but it was nearly evening and the air remained cool.

"I live on Edgevale Street," I said softly.

"OK," Louis replied, his expression a blank.

Then we heard a sound behind us. A girl's voice calling.

We both stopped and turned round.

A girl rode up on a sleek red bike. "Louis!" she called, flashing him a warm smile.

She had curly red hair, which cascaded down her shoulders like a waterfall, and a face full of freckles. She wasn't exactly pretty. Her blue-grey eyes were kind of close together, and she had a short stub of a nose. I guess you'd call her "cute".

She was wearing an oversized green-and-white Glenview High T-shirt with a big G on the front.

"Courtney!" Louis cried. Even though she was smiling at him so warmly, he didn't exactly seem pleased to see her.

"Hi," she said breathlessly, lowering her feet to the road. She glanced at me, then quickly returned her smile to Louis. "What's happening?"

"Bike trouble," Louis replied curtly.

Courtney giggled for some reason.

"This is Abbie," Louis told her. "Abbie . . . uh. . ."

"Kiernan," I said. "Abbie Kiernan. And that's my bike." I pointed to the bike Louis was walking. "I mean, it's my brother's."

"I'm Courtney Bonds," she said and, tossing her red hair behind her shoulders, quickly turned her attention back to Louis. I wasn't sure she had even looked at me.

"Courtney, where are you coming from?" Louis asked. "Up at the falls?"

"Uh-uh." Her smile faded as she shook her head. She blushed. "No way. I've just been riding around. I've been cooped up all day helping my mum with spring-cleaning. So I wanted to get a little exercise."

"Have you seen Emily today?" Louis asked.

"No. I'm going over there tonight," Courtney told him. "Just to hang out."

"Abbie's just moved here," Louis said, suddenly remembering I was still there.

"Oh," Courtney replied, not terribly interested. But then she turned, narrowing her eyes to check me out. "What happened to your bike?" she asked.

"Somebody cut the tyres," I told her. "I really can't believe it."

Courtney glanced dryly at Louis. "I believe it," she muttered under her breath. She flashed Louis a look I couldn't interpret.

Something was going on between the two of them, but I couldn't figure out what.

Was Courtney the person Louis was waiting to meet up at the falls? If she was, wouldn't he ask her why she didn't show up?

I decided he had to be waiting for someone else.

I had the feeling that Louis didn't like Courtney. She kept smiling at him, but I couldn't tell how she felt about him.

"I've got to go," Courtney said suddenly. She fiddled with the gear control on her handlebars. Then she turned to me. "Watch out for Louis," she said through gritted teeth. "Really. He's dangerous. A really dangerous guy."

"Courtney. . . !" Louis started to protest.

But Courtney called out, "Later!" and sped off, standing on her pedals and quickly disappearing round the corner.

"She's weird," Louis said. "She was kidding about me. You know? Courtney and I are old mates."

I saw that Louis was staring at me intently, studying my reaction to what Courtney had said.

"Yeah. I could tell she was joking," I said.

But I wasn't so sure.

She hadn't *looked* as if she were joking. She had looked very serious.

Was she really warning me to stay away from Louis?

Did she mean that he *really* was dangerous?

What a crazy idea.

I glanced once again at Louis. He looked perfectly OK to me.

Better than OK!

With those wild green eyes and that dark, tanned skin, he reminded me suddenly of a tiger.

Tigers are dangerous, I warned myself.

I don't care, I thought.

A short while later, we were standing at the foot of my driveway. We swapped bikes. "Thanks," I said, "for walking me home."

"That's OK. Sorry about your bike."

"D'you want to come in or something?" I offered.

He shook his head. "I've got to get home. See you at school on Monday."

"Yeah. Great," I said. And then I added, "Nice meeting you." It sounded really stupid and phoney.

He ignored it. "And don't forget Friday night," he said, climbing onto his bike.

"I won't. I'm looking forward to it."

*That's for sure!*

I watched him ride away, those long legs pedalling quickly, easily.

I turned and started to drag Jake's bike up the driveway. But then I stopped.

Who was that at the corner?

Someone was waiting under the shadows of a tall hedge. Someone on a bike, keeping close to the hedge. Waiting for Louis.

I stepped back towards the street, squinting hard to see who it was.

Courtney!

She was waiting for him at the corner. She pedalled away from the hedge, out of the shadows, as he came near.

They talked for a moment, close together, side by side on their bikes. And then I watched them ride off together. What's going on here? I wondered. What exactly is going on?

# Four

Jacob Dorsey was the kind of guy who thought it was hilarious to smash Coke cans against his forehead and burp really loudly.

He had long, stringy brown hair that looked as if it hadn't been washed for a month. I spotted a thin gold earring in one ear. His face seemed to be locked in a wide grin, his dark eyes crinkled in laughter. I couldn't imagine a serious expression on his face.

Jacob was tall and lanky and never seemed to stand still. He was very fidgety, very hyper. He bounced around his small, crowded living room, wearing a T-shirt that was too small for him and baggy, faded jeans with enormous holes at the knees, jiggling his shoulders, slapping high fives, shouting and laughing.

At first I couldn't imagine Jacob and Louis being best friends. But after a few hours, I realized that Jacob brought out a lighter side of Louis. Around Jacob, Louis loosened up and became funny, and wild, and loud. Almost as if he were competing with his friend.

I was pretty nervous, being the outsider, the new kid. So I spent a lot of time on the outskirts of the crowd, studying the others.

It was Friday night. Louis had picked me up in a brand-new, silver Volvo and had driven us to Jacob's small box of a house for the usual Friday night blow-out.

Louis seemed pretty relaxed, and I pretended to be. But my stomach was knotted, and my hands were as cold as ice. I mean, it was our first date, and here we were going to a party where he knew everyone and I didn't know a soul.

I had spent at least an hour up in my room puzzling over what to wear. I'd finally ended up in a silky white, long-sleeved top and a short, black skirt over black tights.

As we walked in through the kitchen door, I saw that most of the girls were in jeans, but I didn't care.

Even though it was a cool night out, the house was steamy hot. I spotted about twenty kids, maybe more, jammed into the small living room and spilling into a narrow front hallway.

The music was so loud, the windows rattled. Everyone had to shout to be heard over the noise.

Some couples were dancing near the living room door. A big group of kids hung out in the middle of the living room, laughing and talking. Two couples were pressed together on the narrow stairway leading upstairs, making out, one couple on the bottom step, the other nearly hidden in darkness halfway up the stairs.

Most kids were carrying around cans of Coke, but I saw several with cans of beer. Even though they were away at work, Jacob's parents must know about his Friday night parties, I thought. But I wondered if they knew about the beer.

Holding my hand loosely, Louis led me into the crowded living room. Over the voices and music, I distinctly heard someone ask, "Is that Louis's new girlfriend?" I turned, but I didn't see who said it.

Jacob came bouncing over, grinning. His grin didn't fade as he checked me out. Louis introduced us, giving Jacob a shove.

"Watch out for this jerk," Jacob warned me, shoving Louis back. "He doesn't look it, but he's an animal."

I laughed. But it flashed through my mind that Jacob was the second person to tell me to watch out for Louis.

"You're not animal. You're vegetable," Louis told Jacob.

"You're not even vegetable," Jacob replied. "You're sponge."

"If I'm a sponge, *you're* the stuff you have to wipe up with a sponge!" Louis exclaimed.

The two of them collapsed, laughing.

Shaking his head, Louis said something to me, but I couldn't hear him over the music.

Jacob moved close to me and wrapped a heavy arm round my shoulder. "Don't pay attention to Louis and me," he said, bringing his face close to mine. I smelled beer on his breath. "We're both idiots."

"And proud of it!" Louis declared, grinning. He ran a hand through his hair as his eyes searched the room. "Where's Emily?" he asked Jacob.

Jacob shrugged and slapped a short kid hard on the back, making him spill his Coke on the carpet. The kid didn't even turn round, just kept talking to two other guys.

"Here I am," a girl's voice called from behind me.

I turned to see a tall, dramatic-looking girl with piles of long, curly black hair, big, dark eyes, and dark, lipsticked lips. Despite her black hair and dark features, she had very pale, creamy-white skin. She wore a really short, flowery skirt over black tights. Very sexy.

"Jacob, can't you turn the music down?" she demanded, stepping past me.

"No way." He gave her a goofy grin.

"I can't hear myself think," she shouted.

"Who wants to think?" was Jacob's reply.

"Jacob hates new experiences," Louis commented dryly.

He turned to me. "Abbie, this is Emily Pedderson."

"Hi," Emily shouted over the music. "You're here with *him*?" She pointed to Louis and made a face.

I nodded.

"You must be new here," Emily teased. She tossed her hair back over her shoulder. She seemed to play with her hair a lot, tugging at it, tangling it around her hand, then pushing it off her face.

"Yeah," I said. "I've just moved here."

I turned to Louis, but he and Jacob had disappeared somewhere.

I felt abandoned.

As I looked for him, my eyes stopped on the couple making out at the bottom of the stairs. I couldn't see her face, but I recognized the girl's red hair.

"Courtney!" I declared.

"Have you met Courtney?" Emily asked, stepping close beside me and following my gaze.

"Yeah," I said, staring. "Who's the guy?"

"I don't recognize him," Emily replied. "I don't think he goes to Glenview." She sniggered. "Courtney probably doesn't know his name, either."

I laughed. I liked Emily's nasty sense of humour.

"Some people do aerobics. Courtney does guys," Emily said. And then she turned her eyes to me and her expression grew more intense. "She has a thing for Louis, too. Did you know that?"

"A thing?" I asked. I wasn't sure I'd heard right. It was so noisy.

I couldn't hear what Emily said next.

The two of us found ourselves wandering back towards the kitchen, away from the speakers and the crowd. The kitchen was empty. Someone had spilled a bag of crisps across the worktop.

There was a stack of dirty dishes in the sink. I stepped around a brown puddle of Coke on the floor.

Emily and I leaned against the worktop, chatting and absently picking up the spilled crisps and eating them as we talked. She was nearly 30 centimetres taller than me. She kept complaining that she was overweight, but in my opinion, she was just well-built. I looked like a short little beanpole next to her.

I told her about moving from Ohio, how hard it was to leave my friends behind, to start at a new school so late in the school year.

We both jumped when we heard a loud crash from the living room. "Typical," Emily said, rolling her eyes. "I can't believe Jacob's parents put up with this."

"Jacob's a riot," I said, reaching for another crisp. "He's so funny!"

"Funny-looking," Emily muttered. "Jacob and I have been going out together for about six months. Off and on."

I gazed at her in surprise. I couldn't imagine Jacob and Emily as a couple. "Off and on?" I asked.

"Sometimes I get sick of him," she admitted, glancing to the kitchen doorway. "I mean, he's just never serious. That can be a lot of fun for a while. But sometimes I just want to shake him and say, 'Knock it off. Stop the jokes. Be serious!' He can be a real pain. I mean, he's always getting into trouble at school. Always. . ." She stopped.

"Yeah?" I urged.

She shrugged. "He's OK, I guess. He makes me laugh. And once you really get to know him, he's a good guy." She sighed and tapped a crisp against the worktop until it crumbled. Then she raised her eyes to mine.

"There's something you should know about Louis," she said, lowering her voice, her expression turning solemn.

"Huh? About Louis?"

"Yeah. He's been through a bad time. He—"

She didn't get to finish her sentence. Jacob burst into the room and grabbed her arm. "Come on, Emily – we're all going now."

She pulled out of his grasp. "Going where?"

"To Sportsworld," he replied, tugging her again. He turned to me. "You, too. Come on."

28

"What's Sportsworld?" I asked.

"Batting cages," Emily answered, making a face. "You know. One of those places with basketball courts, and table tennis, and—"

"You can watch me outslug Louis," Jacob said, grinning. "We made a little bet." He put his hands together and bent his knees in a ridiculously exaggerated batting stance. Then he swung all the way around, toppling into the kitchen unit.

"Jacob, how are you going to outslug Louis? You can't outslug *me!*" Emily declared, shaking her head.

"Are you kidding?" He cried, acting as if his feelings were hurt. "You swing like a *girl!*"

"Cute," Emily muttered. "That's really cute." She gave him a hard, playful shove, then followed him to the living room.

I followed Emily, then stopped in the hall way. Across the room, I saw Courtney standing with Louis. She had a hand on his cheek. They were talking with their faces close together.

I think he saw me because he pulled Courtney's hand away from his face and stepped away from her. I made my way across the room, pushing past a circle of kids who were laughing uproariously about something.

"Hey, I lost you," he said as I approached, flashing me a smile. "You remember Courtney?"

I said hi to Courtney, and she nodded. "Did you get your

bike fixed?" she asked, shouting over the laughter across from us.

"It wasn't my bike," I told her. "It was my brother's."

She didn't react. I thought maybe she didn't hear me.

Jacob grabbed my shoulder. "Come on, guys. Let's go!"

Louis flashed me a guilty smile. "Is it OK with you? I sort of made a bet with Jacob."

"Sure," I said. "Sounds like fun."

A few seconds later, about ten of us had piled into two cars, and we were roaring past town towards Sportsworld. I sat beside Louis in the front of his car, with four kids I didn't know in the back.

Louis drove like a madman. He had the radio cranked up as loud as it would go, and he kept careering deliberately from side to side on the road, going at least sixty the whole way.

"Louis!" I shouted when he bumped over the curb into someone's front garden. "Stop it!"

His eyes were wild with excitement, and his grin just grew wider. "I can handle it," he shouted.

He turned the wheel wildly, and the car squealed back into the street.

"Do you always drive like this?" I asked.

He stared into the windscreen, a strange grin fixed on his face, looking almost as if he were hypnotized.

"Louis. . .?"

I was so relieved when we finally reached Sportsworld, a brightly-lit, massive indoor-outdoor sports arena. Louis turned into the car-park, the tyres squealing, and came to an abrupt, bone-jarring stop. I pushed open my car door and practically leaped out, grateful to be in one piece.

To my surprise, Jacob and his group were already going inside. Jacob must be an even crazier driver than Louis, I realized.

I slammed the car door and jogged after Louis, who was already moving across the car-park towards the entrance. "Whew! What a ride!" I cried breathlessly. "That was scary, Louis."

He stopped and turned to me. His smile faded. Those amazing green eyes seemed to burn into mine. "Sometimes I just feel wild," he said. "Like, out of control. You know."

He stood staring at me, hands at his waist, as if waiting for me to reply. But I didn't know what to say. His driving had really frightened me. He *did* seem out of control.

His expression softened. He smiled. "Just kidding," he said. His green eyes seemed to twinkle under the car-park lights. He was so gorgeous! "Come on. Let's go and hit some baseballs."

We started jogging across the car-park to catch up with the others.

I saw Emily up ahead of us, and I suddenly remembered what she had started to tell me in the kitchen: "*There's something you should know about Louis.*"

What had she started to tell me?

Did it have something to do with the way he drove, with his need to get "out of control"?

He seemed to have such drastic mood swings.

Was that what Emily wanted to warn me about?

The batting cages were outdoors, at the back of the building, under daylight-bright lights. I could see a row of eight or ten of them, long canvas-and-wire mesh cages with pitching machines near the far end.

The place was incredibly crowded. Jammed with teenagers and a lot of loud, young, working people. We had to wait for a batting cage. I kept close to Louis, peering through the mesh into the cages, watching helmeted batters take their swings against ninety mph pitches.

"Look at that guy. He's swinging an hour late on every pitch," Louis said, sniggering.

It was a chilly night. It felt more like winter than spring. I shivered. I wished I'd worn a jumper or something.

Louis was shouting encouragement to the guy in the batting cage. He seemed to be enjoying himself. I wondered if he liked me.

Suddenly, I heard a loud, rattling sound above our heads.

Startled, I looked up to see Jacob clinging to the side of the cage, about five metres above the ground. He was holding onto the mesh with one hand, making chimpanzee gestures with his other hand.

"Oh, man!" Louis cried, and then he totally cracked up.

"Get down!" a man cried from somewhere behind us.

"Hey – that's dangerous!" someone else screamed.

"Me Tarzan!" Jacob shouted, climbing to the top of the cage.

"Jacob's so messed up!" Louis exclaimed gleefully. "He's crazy! He'll do *anything*!"

My eye caught Emily, a couple of metres away. She didn't appear at all amused. In fact, her face was bright red, and she looked really embarrassed.

I saw two guys wearing dark blue trousers and white shirts come hurrying over. They must work here, I realized.

"Hey – get down!" one of them waved furiously at Jacob.

"What are you doing?" the other one shouted.

Jacob ignored the two men. "Hey, Louis – join me?" he called down. "You get a better view up here!"

"Do you *believe* him?" Louis asked me, still laughing.

"Come on, man," Jacob called down to Louis. "You chicken?"

Louis stared up at his friend.

"Come on up, wimp!" Jacob called down.

33

The smile faded from Louis's face.

I shuddered.

Louis had the strangest expression on his face. Fear mixed with anger. His entire body went rigid. He stared up at Jacob without moving.

*What is wrong? I* wondered.

*What is Louis thinking about?*

*Why does he suddenly look so strange, so frightening.*

"Hey – chicken face!" Jacob called down, waving his free hand, clinging to the wire mesh with the other. "Chicken face!"

Louis glanced nervously at me. Then he started to call up to Jacob. But Louis's words choked in his throat, and his eyes widened with horror.

As Jacob motioned enthusiastically for Louis to climb up, his hand slipped away from the mesh.

He started to fall.

I watched Jacob plummet all the way down without realizing that the hideous scream I heard the whole time was coming from me.

# Five

I was surrounded by screams and cries of horror.

Louis grabbed my shoulder.

Jacob landed easily on his hands and knees. He rolled over once. Twice. Then climbed to his feet, a goofy, triumphant grin on his face.

"Ta-*daa*!" he sang.

There were groans and loud sighs of relief. Excited voices rang out through the entire area.

The two grim-faced workers came up on either side of Jacob and grabbed his arms.

"Hey, what's the problem?" Jacob demanded. "I mean, what's the problem?"

Louis was still holding tight to my shoulder. I turned to him. He seemed somewhat dazed by the whole thing. "Are you OK?" I asked.

He shook his head. Seemed to snap out of it. "Yeah. I – I was just thinking about something else." Avoiding my eyes, he let go of my shoulder.

Jacob was arguing with the two workers, who wanted to throw him out. Emily came up to me, toying nervously with a thick strand of black hair. "Read any good books lately?" she asked dryly.

"I – I really thought he was going to kill himself this time," Louis said.

"*This* time?" I asked.

"Yeah. He's done it before," Emily told me.

"He does stuff like that all the time," Louis said, shaking his head. "He always lands on his feet."

"Or his head," Emily said with surprising bitterness. "But it never knocks any sense into him."

The two men were leading Jacob out to the exit. I watched Emily run to catch up with them. She seemed really angry and upset. Again I thought what a strange couple Emily and Jacob were. They were so different from each other. And she didn't even seem to like him that much.

Louis had picked a bat up from the bat rack at the side of the cage. He swung it hard once, as if hitting an imaginary pitch. "Looks like our competition is over," he said quietly. "Sorry."

"That's OK," I replied. I was shivering. It was a really cold night.

"Let's go," he said. He tossed the bat to the ground and headed towards the exit.

People were still talking and laughing about Jacob climbing on top of the batting cage. As I followed Louis out, I pictured again the strange expression on his face when Jacob had called for him to climb up, too.

Was it fear?

Was it anger?

Was it jealousy?

His green eyes had filled with such sadness. What had he been thinking of?

I realized I was probably reading too much into it. Louis was probably just afraid for Jacob's safety.

I do that a lot.

"You think too much." That's what my mum always tells me.

I over-analyse everything. I find dark meanings in things that have no meaning at all.

But why was I feeling so troubled as Louis and I made our way to his car?

You're just nervous, Abbie, I told myself. It's your first date with Louis, and you're not sure if he likes you or not.

And why should he like me?

I'd been so quiet all night. I felt like such an outsider among all these kids who'd known each other for ever.

He'll never ask me out again, I thought as I slid into the front seat of the car and pulled the door shut. The leather seat was ice-cold.

Louis started up the car. Two other couples had piled into the back. "Can you turn on some heat?" I asked, folding my arms round myself, trying to get warm.

"No problem," he said, reaching for the dials.

He drove home carefully, keeping below the speed limit. Everyone joked about Jacob and his climb. A boy in the back seat told a story about Jacob breaking into an indoor swimming pool and being caught swimming naked with a bunch of kids. A girl told a story about how Jacob was arrested one night breaking into his own house!

"He's been arrested twenty times!" another boy declared.

Everyone laughed except for Louis. "Jacob's not a criminal," Louis said earnestly. "I mean, he's never been convicted of anything. He always pleads *insanity*!"

Everyone laughed again, including Louis this time.

Laughing and joking, we dropped the other kids off.

I was feeling really good and had finally got warm by the time Louis pulled into my driveway. He left the engine running.

The porch light was on, and the lights were on in my parents' bedroom upstairs. The clock on the dashboard read 11:24. Still pretty early.

I wondered if Louis was going to kiss me.

Gazing at him in the pale white light from the porch, I realized I wanted him to.

His eyes studied the green lights on the dashboard. I wondered what he was thinking.

Was he trying to decide whether or not to kiss me?

Was he nervous, too?

Was he thinking about me at all?

His expression was a total blank. I couldn't read it.

"Well, that's a typical night in Shocklin Falls," he said, turning towards me and smiling.

"I enjoyed it," I said, smiling back.

"Me, too," he said automatically.

Was he going to lean towards me and kiss me?

No.

"See you at school," he said.

"Yeah. OK."

I gave him a few more seconds. But he kept both hands on the wheel. So I pushed open the door and climbed out.

The headlights rolled over the front of the house as I found my keys and pushed open the front door.

I felt disappointed.

I felt like a total idiot.

The front hallway and living room were dark.

Without bothering to turn on the lights, I hung my jacket in the cupboard.

Then I started to make my way through the darkness to the stairs when someone leaped at me and two hands grabbed my shoulders from behind.

# Six

Uttering a silent gasp, I stumbled forward into the banister.

I heard footsteps pad across the floor.

"Goggles!" I cried out in a choked whisper.

I clicked on the hall light. The stupid cat was standing at my feet, staring up at me.

"Goggles, how many times do I have to tell you not to scare me like that?" I asked, picking him up.

He purred excitedly.

I touched his nose to mine.

"Don't jump on me," I told him for the thousandth time. "I don't have nine lives like you do."

I hugged him close, rubbing my hand down his soft, white fur. "You don't understand a word I'm saying, do you, stupid?"

He purred contentedly as I stroked his back. Then he

swiped at me with his paw, his way of telling me he'd had enough affection.

I set him down and he padded away.

Goggles has some bad habits. Jumping on people in the dark is one of his worst. But I love him just the same. He is so cute with all that fluffy white fur and those big, serious blue eyes.

I had started up the stairs, thinking about Louis, when my mother's voice interrupted my thoughts. "Abbie, is that you?"

Who *else* would it be?

"Yes, it's me," I called.

She appeared on the landing, her hair down, wearing a long pink nightie. "How was your date?"

"Fine."

I always give the same reply to that question. What does she expect – *details*?

"What did you do?" my mother asked, yawning loudly.

"Went to a party," I told her, starting the climb up the stairs. "Just a lot of kids hanging around."

"That's nice," she replied sleepily. "See you in the morning." She disappeared into her room.

A few minutes later, I was changed, in bed, thinking about Louis.

Once again, I heard the girl at Jacob's house saying, "*That's Louis's new girlfriend.*" I wondered if I *was* Louis's new girlfriend.

I wondered if he'd ever ask me out again.

Before I realized it, I drifted into a sound sleep. If I dreamed about Louis, I didn't remember it in the morning.

I ran into Emily at school on Monday morning. We talked for a while between classes. It turned out we were in the same geography class.

I decided I really liked her. I hoped we could become good friends.

During lunch break, I spotted Emily at a table in the corner of the canteen and I carried my tray over to have lunch with her.

We talked about our geography coursework. Emily and the others in the class had a real head start on me. They'd already been researching for three weeks. I knew I'd be spending a lot of time in the library and in the computer room, typing up all my research, trying to catch up with the others in the class.

Eventually, the conversation came round to Louis.

"Where'd you meet him?" Emily asked, taking a forkful of her salad.

"Up at the falls," I replied.

She put down her fork. Her mouth dropped open in surprise. "Huh? Where?"

"At the falls," I repeated, startled by her reaction.

She tossed a thick strand of black hair back over her shoulder and stared at me, studying my face as if trying to determine if I were telling the truth.

"I was bike riding," I said. "You know. Exploring. I followed the bike path up to the falls and—"

"I really can't believe Louis would go up there," Emily interrupted, still staring at me intently. She picked up her fork and started tapping it nervously against the canteen tray.

"What's wrong, Emily?" I asked.

Her dark eyes narrowed. "Are we talking about the same falls?"

"Is there more than one?" I asked innocently.

"No." She shook her head. "I just can't believe Louis would ever go up there again. I mean, after what happened."

I set down my slice of pizza. A sliver of cheese stuck to my thumb. I chewed it off. "Did something bad happen up there?" I asked. "To Louis?"

Emily nodded. "Yeah. A few months ago. Last January."

She stopped, then started again. "I guess I might as well tell you about it. I mean, everyone knows. It's not like a secret or anything. That's for sure."

"What?" I cried impatiently. "What? What? Stop being so mysterious. You're driving me crazy!"

"I don't think you'll like it once you hear it," Emily replied softly.

"*What*'s driving you crazy?" demanded a voice behind us.

I turned to see Courtney standing right behind me, a loaded-up lunch tray in her hands. She put the tray down beside me, across from Emily, and sat down. "You both look so serious," she said, moving the plates around on her tray. "What are you talking about? Your hair?"

"Our geography coursework," Emily answered quickly, casting me a quick glance that told me not to contradict with the truth.

Courtney brushed her red hair back over the shoulder of her green T-shirt and concentrated on pushing the straw into her juice carton. "We don't have coursework in Curtis's class," she told them. "We have a killer exam instead."

"I think I'd rather have the exam," I said, taking a bite of the small square of pizza. "I'm getting such a late start."

"You wouldn't want *this* exam," Courtney insisted, picking up a hamburger, watching the grease drizzle from the bun. "It has really easy, specific questions, like, 'Compare and contrast every country on earth.'"

Emily and I laughed appreciatively. That was a pretty good exam question.

We chatted about teachers and classes. All the while I was dying to hear what Emily had started to tell me about Louis. But it was obvious Emily didn't want to talk about it while Courtney was around.

What could it be? I wondered, my mind spinning with wild ideas.

Why was Emily so surprised that Louis was up at the falls?

What happened up there?

We were nearly finished with our lunches when I felt a tap on my shoulder. I looked up to find Louis smiling down at me. He was wearing a pale blue jumper over dark, straight-legged jeans. He looked really great.

"Hi!" I cried, unable to hide my surprise. I'd looked for him all day, but hadn't seen him.

"How's it going?" he asked, glancing quickly at Emily, then returning his attention to me. He pointed to my tray. "You like cardboard pizza?"

"It's my favourite," I replied. "It's going OK, I guess. I keep getting lost. This school is so much bigger than my old school."

"Have you seen Jacob?" Louis asked Emily.

She made a face. "He's doing lunchtime detention."

Louis laughed. "What for?"

Emily rolled her eyes. "He said a rude word to Mrs Kelman."

"Jacob only knows rude words," Louis said, sniggering. "Abbie, have you got your new bike yet?"

I nodded. "I got a used one. The new ones were too expensive. It's excellent, though. Twenty-one speed."

Louis leaned close. "Great. Want to go riding on Saturday afternoon?"

I had promised my dad I'd help him unpack some of the boxes in the garage, but I knew I could get out of it. "Yeah. Great," I said. "Come and pick me up, OK?"

"OK." Louis disappeared as quickly as he had appeared.

I felt really happy. Maybe Louis *didn't* think I was a total drip. Maybe he *did* like me.

My smile faded when I caught Courtney's expression. She was biting her lower lip, her features in a tight frown. She was suddenly pale white, sickly white.

"Courtney – are you feeling OK?" I blurted out.

"No, not really," she replied weakly. She let the rest of her hamburger drop to the tray and scooted her chair back. "I think this food has made me ill or something."

"Can I help you. . .?" I started. But she jumped to her feet and hurried out of the canteen without looking back.

"D'you think we should go with her?" I asked Emily.

Emily shook her head. "She'll be fine." She'd been toying with her salad the whole time, but had hardly eaten a bite.

"Aren't you starving?" I asked.

Emily nodded. "Yeah. But I've got to lose weight. I hate having a boyfriend who's skinnier than I am."

"I think you're just about perfect," I blurted out, and then was immediately embarrassed that I'd said it. But it was true.

I'd give anything to look like Emily instead of having this short, little-boyish figure.

Emily picked up her tray and got to her feet. "Ready?"

I nodded. "Yeah. But you've got to finish what you were telling me. About Louis."

Her expression turned serious. "OK, Abbie. I'll tell you," she said softly. "But it may change everything. Really."

"I don't understand," I said. "Change what?"

"The way you feel about Louis, for one thing," Emily replied. "You see, it's about the girl who died. Have you heard about it?"

*Died?*

The word stuck in my mind. It stayed there, echoing as if it would never fade away.

*Died?*

What girl?

We deposited our trays on the dirty-tray counter. The floor seemed to tilt beneath my feet. The fluorescent lights above us appeared to flash like bright explosions.

Maybe I *don't* want to hear this, I thought, shutting my eyes till the flashing stopped.

"No. I haven't heard about it," I told Emily, my voice shaky.

I followed her out of the canteen. She led us up the stairs and down the hall that led to the principal's office in the front of the building.

The hall was crowded and noisy, filled with kids who had finished their lunch and were messing around, waiting for the bell to ring.

I didn't pay any attention to them. I followed Emily, wondering where she was leading us, what she was going to tell me. And as we walked, my stomach tightened with dread. My hands turned cold. My heart began to race.

"*It may change everything,*" Emily had said.

*Everything.*

What could she be talking about?

We turned a corner. We were near the front entrance. The principal's office stood diagonally across from the big double doorways. And in the wall beside the office stood a large glass display case, the kind usually used for showing off sports trophies.

Emily stopped in front of the display case. She pushed her thick black hair back behind her head with both hands and peered into my eyes. "This is the girl who died," she said, gesturing to the glass case. "She died up at the falls."

I swallowed hard and stared into the case.

It was empty except for a single photograph. A colour enlargement of a school photo.

It was a photo of a pretty girl. She had it all. Bright blonde hair. Flashing blue eyes. High cheekbones like a model. A beautiful smile revealing perfect white teeth.

The photo was draped with black crêpe.

Under the photo stood a small black tag. It read: 1992–2009.

I stared into the girl's eyes. They stared coldly back at me.

After a few seconds, I had to look away.

"She died?" I asked Emily in a tight, shrill voice. "Who is she? I mean, who was she?"

"That's Phoebe," Emily answered softly. "Louis's girlfriend."

# Seven

I stared through the glass at the photo of Phoebe.

I stared at those round blue eyes, at that perfect smile, at the honey-blonde hair, brushed casually back, so soft against her perfect skin.

The black crêpe draped round the photo didn't belong.

She was so light, so pretty, so . . . happy.

I couldn't picture her wearing black.

She shouldn't be in this dark, heavy case, I thought. She shouldn't be here with her dates under her photo.

The display case was like a glass casket. I was staring into Phoebe's casket.

Staring at her smiling face, her pretty blue eyes.

I turned away with a violent shudder. I felt that I was somehow invading her privacy.

"She was Louis's girlfriend?" I asked Emily.

Emily nodded.

I wanted to ask more. A hundred questions flooded my mind. I wanted to know everything about her. I wanted to know what she was like. And I wanted to know how she died.

And why did Emily say it would change my idea of Louis?

But the bell rang right over our heads. The hall was filled with kids stampeding noisily to class.

Emily gave me a quick wave and hurried away, leaving me standing there.

Standing there with Phoebe.

My eyes locked on Phoebe's once again. And as I stared, the voices and laughter echoing down the hall faded away.

Phoebe and I were alone.

What is your story, Phoebe? I asked silently. What happened to you up at the falls?

She stared back at me through the glass.

1992–2009.

The dates seemed to shimmer and then blur.

Was that *sadness* I detected deep in those blue eyes? Sadness behind the posed smile?

I had to force myself to turn away.

To my surprise, the hall was nearly empty. The second bell was about to ring, and I hadn't even collected my books.

How long had I been standing there?

I knew I had to talk to Emily, had to find out the answers

to all my questions. Avoiding the display case, I jogged past it and headed to my locker.

I'll call Emily later, I decided.

I'll make her tell me everything.

The afternoon seemed to drag on for days. I was very distracted. I don't think I heard a word anyone said.

After school, I spent a couple of long, dreary hours in the computer room, typing up my geography research. Normally, I enjoy doing research. I like digging around in old books for facts and information. It's sort of like being an archaeologist.

But I had joined the class so late, and I was so far behind everyone else, I felt really pressured. Glenview High seemed a lot more intense than my old school. Also, I wasn't used to the kind of computers they had in the computer room, so I kept making mistakes.

That night, struggling to concentrate on my maths homework, I found myself still thinking about Phoebe, still eager to unravel the mystery about her. I kept calling Emily all evening. At first, there was no answer. And then the line was busy for hours.

So frustrating!

I didn't get to talk to Emily about Phoebe until lunch the next day. I forced Emily to gulp down her lunch. (She was only having a salad anyway.) And then I dragged her to the display case at the front of the building.

"You have to tell me the whole story," I insisted, staring at the photograph, finding myself searching once again for the sadness in Phoebe's eyes. "What happened to her?"

Emily hesitated. She leaned against the tile wall, toying thoughtfully with a thick strand of black hair, wrapping it and unwrapping it round her finger. "You sure you want to know?"

"Yeah. I'm sure," I replied impatiently. "Tell me what happened."

"No one really knows," Emily said, still fingering her hair. "I mean, no one knows for sure."

I groaned. "Start at the beginning," I urged.

Emily waited for a group of cheerleaders to pass. They were in their green-and-white uniforms, laughing and playfully shoving each other into the walls.

When they had turned the corner, Emily let go of her hair and took a step closer to me. "It happened last January. It was a really warm day for January. Phoebe and Louis went bike riding up to the falls. Somehow, Phoebe and her bike went over the falls. And she died."

I gasped and shut my eyes. "Over the falls?"

I tried not to picture it. It was so horrible.

The falls were so steep. The water crashed straight down. Down onto those jagged black rocks.

54

"Over the falls," Emily repeated softly.

"But, Louis. . ." I started. I didn't really know what I wanted to say.

"Louis told everyone he had left Phoebe for a minute or two," Emily continued, staring into the display case, her hands knotted into tight fists at her sides. "Louis said he saw someone. Back on the bike path. Or, he thought he saw someone. Anyway," Emily sighed, "he went to see who it was. And when he came back. . ."

She didn't finish her sentence.

I swallowed hard, staring into the display case. Phoebe's photo was just a blur of colour to me now, all greens and pinks, surrounded by black.

"When he came back, Phoebe was gone?" I managed to ask.

Emily nodded. "Louis looked for her. And then he saw her bike. Down below. All mangled. It had caught on the rocks."

"And Phoebe?" I asked, my voice choked with the horror of it all.

"They dragged her body out downriver," Emily said in a whisper. "Two days later. She was cut to pieces."

I gasped. "Someone had cut her?"

Emily shook her head grimly. "The police said she'd been cut up by all the rocks."

I tried to focus on the photo in the display case, but it

wouldn't come clear. I rested one hand against the wall to steady myself.

Such a horrible story.

And to think that I'd just been up at the falls. With Louis. I could picture it all so clearly. I could hear the roar of the falls in my ears. I could see the winding cycle path and the woods behind it.

I could see the cliff-edge over the falls.

I could see the black, pointed rocks in the river below.

I could see it all.

I turned to Emily, who had folded her arms over her chest. "Why did she kill herself?" I managed to ask.

"What makes you think she killed herself?" Emily asked with surprising emotion.

"Huh?" I gaped at her, trying to figure out what she was trying to tell me.

The principal, Mr Velasquez, passed by, dabbing a wet handkerchief over a dark stain on his yellow tie. He glanced up as he walked by us, nodded solemnly, and disappeared into his office, still working on the tie.

"I was Phoebe's best friend," Emily confided. "I thought she was perfectly happy." She sighed and lowered her eyes to the floor. Then she added, "I guess you never really know another person. Even a close friend. You never really know what's in their mind."

"But—"

"The police decided it was suicide," Emily interrupted, still staring at her white trainers. "In case you didn't already know it, Louis's parents are very rich. They got the police investigation to end very quickly."

Emily's words stunned me. I raised my hands to my forehead and rubbed my throbbing temples.

"But no one suspected Louis – *did* they?" I asked, my voice choked with emotion.

"No, not really," Emily replied reluctantly. She raised her eyes to mine. "But there were stories. You know. You know how rumours get started."

"What kind of rumours?" I demanded.

"Just rumours," Emily replied edgily. "Rumours that Louis and Phoebe had had a big fight. That Louis wanted to break up with her and start going out with someone else."

"Someone else?"

"Well . . . some kids saw his car parked in Courtney's driveway one night."

I stared hard at Emily, trying to understand what she was saying, trying to read her mind, to figure out what she really believed had happened.

"Emily, *you* don't think that Louis killed Phoebe – do you?" I asked.

"No. Of course not," she replied quickly.

Too quickly.

She grabbed my arm and moved her face close to mine. "But I'd be careful, Abbie," she whispered.

Careful?

What did she mean?

"I'd be really careful," she repeated in a low whisper, gripping my arm tightly.

"Emily. . . ?"

"I've got to run," she said, letting go. "Later, OK?"

Before I could reply, she started jogging down the hallway.

*Be careful?*

Her words remained in my mind.

What did she mean?

Did she mean to be careful of Louis?

Did she really think that Louis murdered Phoebe? Pushed her over the falls? Then got his parents to hush it up with the police?

No. No way.

She *said* she didn't think that Louis had killed Phoebe.

So why was Emily warning me to be careful?

I shoved my hands into my jeans pockets and tried to stop from trembling. I wanted to walk away, to go to my locker, to go to my next class, to think about something else.

*Anything* else.

But Phoebe wouldn't let me go.

Her black-draped photo beckoned to me, called me, pulled me in. I stood there staring through the glass at her.

Emily had told me the whole story.

But she hadn't really told me any of it.

There is a story behind the story, isn't there, Phoebe? I asked silently.

There are secrets you haven't revealed.

Secrets you may never reveal.

I stood there in the brightly-lit hallway, hands shoved into my pockets, and stared at the photo as if searching the pretty face for the answers it hid.

I don't know how long I stared at it.

And I don't know how long it took me to realize that someone else had joined me. Someone else was standing right beside me, so close that his shoulder pressed against mine.

I don't know how long it took me to realize he was staring intently at me as I stared at Phoebe.

"She didn't kill herself," he said.

# Eight

"What did you say?" I cried, startled.

I took a step away from him and studied his face. He wore round glasses with thin gold frames. He was short, shorter than me, and thin like a pencil. He had a lean face, with intense brown eyes, exaggerated by the glasses. His brown hair was short and spiky.

Taking another step back, I saw that he was wearing a green-and-black-striped polo shirt over jeans.

He flashed me a nervous smile and blinked two or three times behind his glasses.

"Hi," he said shyly. "You were in the computer room after school yesterday, right?" He had a surprisingly deep voice. He kept blinking nervously and shifting his books as he talked.

"Yeah," I replied.

"I was there, too. Did you see me?"

I shook my head and smiled at him. "I was concentrating

so hard on typing up my research, I didn't see anybody," I confessed.

His narrow face fell in disappointment.

"My name's Ryan," he said shyly.

"Hi," I said. "Is that your first name or last?"

"I have two last names," he replied, a smile slowly spreading across his face. "I mean, both my names *could* be last names. Ryan is my first name. Ryan Baker."

I laughed. "Do you have a last name for a middle name?"

"No," he replied seriously. "I don't have a middle name. Just two first names."

"I'm Abbie Kiernan," I told him.

"I know," he blurted out, then blushed. "I mean, I heard someone say your name. You've just started here, right?"

"Right," I said. I glanced up at the clock outside the principal's office. The bell was going to ring any second.

He cleared his throat nervously and turned his gaze to Phoebe's picture. "She was a really good friend of mine," he confided, his face completely expressionless. "I mean, we were *really* good friends."

"Yeah?" I didn't know what to say.

"We didn't go out or anything," Ryan continued, staring hard into the display case. "We were just really good friends. In fact. . ." He hesitated. He changed his mind about what he was going to say.

"What a terrible thing," I muttered awkwardly.

Something about Ryan made me feel very awkward and uncomfortable. I guess it was his nervousness.

"You've heard the whole story?" he asked, staring at Phoebe.

"Yeah. Most of it," I replied.

"Well, she didn't kill herself!" he cried with surprising vehemence.

That's what I'd *thought* he'd said before.

*She didn't kill herself.*

"How do you know?" I blurted out, taking another step away from him.

"I know it," he snapped. He blushed again.

The bell rang, startling us both.

I hesitated. He didn't move. "I guess we should get to class," I said, eager to get away from him.

He nodded, still not moving. "Are you busy on Saturday, Abbie? Would you like to go to the cinema or something?"

His question caught me by surprise. My mouth dropped open. I gaped at him as if I didn't understand what he was asking. I must have looked like a total idiot.

Why did Ryan make me feel so awkward?

"I guess you're probably busy," he muttered unhappily. "Well, some other time, maybe."

I remembered that I *did* have a date with Louis on Saturday, for the afternoon, at least.

"Yeah. Some other time," I said, feeling foolish. "Nice meeting you, Ryan."

He mumbled something, avoiding my eyes, and hurried away. I watched him disappear round the corner.

"Strange guy," I said out loud.

Then, taking one last glance at Phoebe's photo, I turned away and hurried to my lesson.

The afternoon was pretty much of a disaster.

I had done the wrong pages in the maths workbook, and Mr Woolrich insisted on making fun of me in front of the entire class.

Really sensitive guy, Mr Woolrich.

And then I was trying to drink from the water fountain next to the gym, and the water went down the wrong way and, in front of a big crowd, some boy I'd never seen before started slapping my back to help me stop choking.

Of course it didn't help. And I was totally mortified.

I was pretty well wrecked by the time I got up to the computer room after school. I probably should have just gone home and vegged out with some TV for the rest of the afternoon. But I still had several pages of research to type up.

The computer room was empty except for a couple of girls typing furiously away in the back. I looked for Ryan and was relieved to see that he wasn't there.

Just thinking about him made me uncomfortable.

Maybe I'm prejudiced against guys who are shorter than I am, I thought.

No. That wasn't the reason he made me feel awkward. It was just that he was so nervous and awkward himself.

And he was saying such revealing, frightening things to me, a total stranger.

"*Phoebe didn't kill herself.*"

Why did he say that to me? Was he deliberately trying to scare me or something?

I shook my head hard as if trying to shake Ryan out of my mind. Then I found my disk in the file and inserted it in the computer I had used before in the front row.

The computer whirred, and the screen went black.

"Hey, wait!" I cried out loud.

Where were all the notes I had typed in yesterday?

I must have done something wrong. They must be here. They've *got* to be here.

"I *hate* these stupid computers," I muttered under my breath.

I turned off the machine and started again.

The name of my file appeared at the top.

But the rest of the screen was blank.

Completely blank.

My throat tightened. I suddenly felt sick.

"Where are you hiding my stuff?" I asked the computer.

I stared at the blank screen in angry disbelief.

My notes – all of my work – was gone.

Erased.

A heavy, sinking feeling in my stomach, I hit the keys, moving the screen down, page after page.

All erased. All a total blank.

Page after page after page.

"No!" I uttered a cry of total exasperation.

This can't be happening.

Wait.

There was something at the end of the file.

Two lines of type.

I was so upset, it took a while to focus on the words.

As I read the lines, the sinking feeling spread over my entire body, and I felt cold all over.

At the bottom of the screen were two short sentences:

STAY AWAY FROM LOUIS.
IT COULD SAVE YOUR LIFE.

# Nine

It wasn't an accident, I realized.

My notes weren't erased by accident.

The computer didn't do it. A person did it.

Someone erased my work, then typed the threatening message at the end.

"Who?" I cried, not realizing I was talking out loud.

I turned and saw the two girls in the back look up at me.

I clicked off the computer and, leaving my disk in the machine, shoved my books into my school bag and burst out of the room.

I was breathing hard. My temples throbbed.

I ran down the corridor, my trainers thudding loudly on the hard floor, then down the stairs.

*Who did that to me?* I wondered.

All my hard work. And I was already so far behind everyone else.

I felt like crying. But I forced myself not to.

*Who did it?*

I ran past the empty classrooms, past a caretaker carrying two large grey rubbish bins, past rows of silent lockers.

I came to an abrupt halt in front of Phoebe's display case.

*Don't stop*, I told myself.

But something kept me from running further.

Phoebe stared out at me.

Her smile had changed.

She was *warning* me. Warning me to stay away from Louis.

No!

"Don't get weird, Abbie," I scolded myself aloud.

I forced my eyes away from the photograph and hurried round the corner.

Laughter. Up ahead.

I saw Emily leaning against her locker, books and notebooks at her feet. And I saw Jacob standing close to her.

They were laughing giddily about something.

They stopped when they saw me approaching.

"Got to go," Jacob said, reaching down and picking up some of the books and handing them to Emily. "How's it going?" he called to me.

"Peachy," I replied sarcastically. "Just peachy."

But Jacob had taken off, waving to Emily without waiting for my answer.

"Hi, Abbie. What's your problem?" Emily asked, stooping to pick up the rest of her stuff.

"Somebody erased all my work," I blurted out breathlessly.

Emily straightened up, leaving her books on the floor. "Huh?"

I repeated what I'd said. Her mouth dropped open. She shook her head.

I told her about the warning at the end of the file, telling me to stay away from Louis.

Her expression turned thoughtful. She tugged at her hair. "Who would do such a mean thing?" she asked.

I shrugged. "I don't even *know* anyone," I wailed. "This is only my second day in this stupid school!"

"D'you want to go somewhere and talk about it?" Emily offered.

"I don't know," I replied miserably. "I think I'll just go home. I'm having a bad day, and. . ."

I stopped when I saw Louis turn the corner. He had his head down and was loping along quickly. A smile spread across his face when he spotted me.

"Hey – hi!" he shouted. He came hurrying up to us, his bag over one shoulder, a tennis racquet in a blue case in one hand. "What are you guys doing here so late?"

"Jacob had detention, and I had to get some notes from him," Emily explained.

"Wow. You're in major trouble if you need notes from Jacob!" Louis teased her.

"They were *my* notes. I had to get them back from him," Emily said. She stooped and began picking up her stuff from the floor.

Louis turned his attention to me. "What are *you* doing?"

I felt a sudden tremor of fear.

The warning on my computer screen flashed in my mind. And I suddenly saw Phoebe's face.

*Did you kill her, Louis?*

The question popped into my mind.

I stared at Louis. Was I really afraid of him?

No.

The feeling of fear quickly faded.

He smiled at me warmly, running his free hand back shyly through his thick hair. His green eyes seemed to smile, too.

Louis is no killer, I decided.

"I was up in the computer room," I told him. "But something's happened to my disk. All my work has been erased."

"I'm not surprised," Louis replied.

"Huh?" I stared at him, startled by his matter-of-fact words. Emily glanced up at him, too.

"Those old Macs are terrible," Louis explained, bouncing the tennis racquet against his shoulder. "Some of them are practically falling apart. My cousin goes to Franklin Heights, and he says they have loads of brand-new Macs in their computer room."

"Well, I don't know if it was the computer's fault or not, but all my work is lost," I said unhappily, deciding not to tell him about the warning someone had typed at the end of the file.

Emily shoved the books and stuff inside her locker, slammed the door, and locked it. "I've got to run." She turned to Louis. "What are you doing hanging around so late? Did you have detention, too?"

He raised his tennis racquet. "Tennis team practice," he told her. "We're going to be champions this year."

"In your dreams," Emily muttered sarcastically.

Louis's grin grew wider. "No. Really."

"I've got to go," Emily said, turning to me. "If I'm late for work, they yell at me a lot."

"See you," I said, thinking about my lost notes.

"D'you want to do something on Saturday afternoon?" she called back to me, halfway down the hall. "I have a class in the morning. But later we could drive to the mall or something?"

"I can't," I called back. "Louis and I are going to test out my new bike. Want to come along?"

"No thanks. I'm in a shopping mood. See you around." And she disappeared out the side door.

Louis and I were alone now, alone in the long, empty hallway. He spun the racquet handle in his hand.

I struggled to think of something to say.

I wondered if I should tell him that I knew about Phoebe.

Somehow this didn't seem like the time or the place.

Maybe I'll tell him on Saturday, I thought. Or maybe not.

I mean, what's the point of saying anything about it?

And what could I possibly say?

"D'you want to walk me home?" I asked, my nervous stammer suddenly returning. "Or would you like me to walk *you* home?"

He smiled, but shook his head. "Can't. I've got to get back to practice. I just came in to make a phone call."

"OK," I said, shifting my bag on my shoulders. "See you later. I'm really looking forward to Saturday."

"Me, too," he said, twirling the tennis racquet.

We walked together to the side door, our footsteps echoing in the empty corridor. He started to push open the door, then stopped.

He hesitated. Then, to my surprise, he leaned down and

71

kissed me, pushing his lips against mine, softly at first, then harder.

I was so stunned, I swallowed noisily.

Looking over his shoulder as we kissed, I suddenly saw something.

A flash of colour.

Someone watching us from the corner where the hallway turned.

I backed away from Louis to see better.

Whoever it was pulled back out of sight.

But not before I saw a flash of red hair.

Courtney!

"Come here, Goggles. Come and sit on my lap."

I'd been calling to the stubborn cat for ten minutes, but he refused to budge. He just sat in the doorway to the TV room, staring up at me in the armchair as if I were crazy.

"OK, stay there," I said crossly, giving up. "Be as unfriendly as you like, you fat furry mop."

As soon as I said that, the contrary animal hurried across the room and leaped into my lap.

I laughed. "I should've used reverse psychology on you before," I told him, stroking the soft, white fur on his back. Goggles put up with me for about a minute, then scampered away.

It was Friday night. I was alone in the house and feeling restless. My parents had gone to a party at the college, and Jake had a sleepover at one of his new friend's houses.

I tapped my fingers against the arm of the leather chair, trying to decide what to do. There was nothing on TV.

I knew I should do more research for my geography coursework. But I just wasn't in the mood. I mean, who does homework on a Friday night?

"Goggles, where are you?" I called.

Then I scolded myself for pestering the cat. Goggles wasn't very good company.

I stood up, thinking maybe I'd do something with my hair. Wash it, then try to style it like that model I saw in a picture in *Sugar*.

As I started for the doorway, the photo of Phoebe flashed into my mind. I saw her hair. It was as blonde as mine, but prettier and wavier. It fell so casually, so naturally. It looked as if she didn't have to fuss with it at all.

She *doesn't* have to fuss with it any more, I thought grimly.

She's dead.

I tried not to, but for the hundredth time I pictured poor Phoebe plunging over the falls with her bike, screaming all the way down. Until she hit the sharp rocks with a sickening *splat*.

No!

Why did I keep imagining that horrifying scene again and again?

Why couldn't I stop thinking about her, about her hideous death?

Think about something pleasant, I told myself.

Force Phoebe out of your thoughts. Think about something good that's happening in your life.

And then I thought of Louis.

I wondered what he was doing tonight. I wondered if he was sitting around the house, as bored as I was.

Go ahead. Call him, I urged myself.

I dropped back onto the big armchair and picked up the phone from the end table beside me.

I hesitated.

I suddenly felt nervous.

Go ahead, Abbie, I thought. Call him.

What's the big deal?

Holding the receiver, I realized I didn't have Louis's number. I found it in the phone book and I quickly punched it in before I lost my nerve.

It rang once. Twice.

I realized I was squeezing the receiver so tightly, my hand hurt. So I loosened my grip.

Three rings.

He isn't home, I thought, disappointed. No one's home.

Someone picked up in the middle of the fourth ring. "Hello?"

"Uh . . . Mrs M-Morgan?" I stammered.

"Is that you, Courtney?" Mrs Morgan asked, sounding surprised. "Hasn't Louis picked you up yet? He left for your house a long time ago."

I froze.

My blood seemed to stop flowing. My body turned to granite.

I was a statue. A cold statue.

"Courtney?" Louis's mother asked.

"Sorry. I have the wrong n-number," I managed to say. And I slammed down the receiver.

*Louis is out with Courtney tonight?*

I scolded myself for feeling so hurt.

He had a perfect right to go out with Courtney, after all. It wasn't like Louis and I. . .

We weren't. . .

He and I never said. . .

I took a deep breath and held it.

I tried to chill out, to stop the angry, upset thoughts from careering through my mind.

I looked down and saw Goggles staring at me from the doorway with those big blue cat eyes.

"Louis's out with Courtney tonight," I told the cat.

I jumped a mile as the phone rang. Goggles scampered away.

I picked it up before the second ring.

A harsh, raspy voice began talking before I even said hello.

"*Computers don't lie*," someone whispered loudly. "*Stay away from Louis Morgan. One dead girlfriend is enough.*"

# Ten

I couldn't get to sleep after that. The raspy, whispering voice kept repeating its crude warning in my mind.

I hadn't been frightened at first.

Sitting in the TV room, staring at the phone beside me, I'd been more angry than frightened.

Did someone really think they could scare me away from Louis by whispering stupid threats over the phone?

The more I thought about it, though, the more frightened I became.

The phone caller knew about the computer. He or she obviously was the one who erased my coursework.

And did the caller also slash Jake's bike tyres that afternoon when I met Louis?

Whoever it was knew how to reach me, knew where I lived.

I shuddered.

I suddenly remembered a film I'd seen on TV where a babysitter is alone in a house, and she starts getting frightening phone calls – and the caller is upstairs, *right in the house with her*!

I got up and scurried round the house, making sure the doors were locked.

As if that would do any good if someone really wanted to get me.

"It's just a practical joke," I told myself out loud. My trembling voice didn't sound very reassuring.

And again I thought of Phoebe.

She was *really* dead. No practical joke.

Later, I went to bed and couldn't get to sleep.

The shadows on my ceiling looked like dark, pointed rocks.

I stared up at them wide-eyed, feeling the fear choke my throat, hearing the whispered threat over the phone, the raspy voice like water rushing over the falls.

Somehow I eventually fell asleep.

The next morning, I called Emily right after breakfast. I *had* to talk to someone.

"I'm rushing out," she said, surprised to hear from me so early. "I have this stupid electrical engineering class on Saturday mornings."

"You have *what*?" I demanded, certain that I hadn't heard her correctly.

"You heard me," she replied, groaning. "It's a beginner's course in electrical wiring and stuff. It's two hours every Saturday morning. You see, Courtney thinks that girls should know how to do stuff like that. You know. Have skills. And she talked me into taking the class with her."

"How did she ever do that?" I asked.

"Well, the instructor's this really cute guy. . ." Emily started. She sighed. "I don't know. We've only been doing it for a couple of weeks. It's kind of interesting. Circuits and stuff."

"Weird," I said.

"What's up?" she asked.

"I got this call last night," I said. I told her about the frightening call. The threat.

"That's really gross!" Emily exclaimed. "Did you tell your parents?"

"Well . . . no," I replied.

"Maybe you should tell them," Emily urged. "Whoever this nut is, he might be serious. I think your parents should know."

'What makes you think it's a *he*?" I asked.

Emily was silent for a moment. I could practically hear her brain working over the phone line. "Why? Who do you think it is?" she asked finally.

"Courtney, maybe," I said.

I hadn't really thought about it before that second. I hadn't really suspected Courtney.

But, suddenly, the whispered, raspy voice sounded a lot like Courtney's to me.

"Courtney?" Emily sounded stunned. "Hey, Abbie, I don't think so."

"But, Emily—"

"Courtney's OK," Emily interrupted. "You shouldn't trust first impressions. She's really OK."

"Well, you know her better than I do," I said reluctantly. "But something about the whispered voice. . ."

"Come on. Why would Courtney try to scare you away from Louis?" Emily demanded.

"Well, for one thing, they went out together last night," I said.

"Huh?"

Emily sounded really shocked.

"Are you sure?" she asked breathlessly.

"Yeah, I'm sure." I told Emily about my phone call to Louis's house, and how Mrs Morgan mistook me for Courtney.

'Wow," Emily kept repeating. "Wow."

"How come you're so surprised?" I demanded.

It took her a while to answer. "It's sort of a long story," she said. "I'm just surprised, that's all. I'll have to ask Courtney all about their date at our class. I'll tell you about it later. I'm late."

"But, Emily. . ."

"Are you still going bike riding with Louis this afternoon?" she asked.

"Yeah. I guess."

"Well, be careful, OK?" And then Emily hung up.

*Be careful?*

I stared at the humming phone receiver. What did she mean?

Be careful of *what*? Of Louis?

Louis arrived a little before two. I watched from the living room window as he sped up our driveway on his bike and leaped off while it was still going, letting the bike topple to the grass.

He didn't see me. I watched him from the window as he pulled down his pale blue hoody and pushed back his hair with both hands.

It was kind of fun spying on him.

He's so good-looking, I thought. He should be in Hollywood starring on TV shows.

I suddenly remembered something my mum had said a long time ago about not hanging around with boys who were better-looking than I was.

It's funny the things that pop into your mind for no reason at all.

The front doorbell rang. I hurried across the room and pulled open the door.

Louis seemed really glad to see me. We talked for a few minutes, just making small talk. I pulled a long green blade of grass from his hair. "How'd you get this?" I asked, twirling it in my fingers.

"Mowing the lawn this morning," he groaned. "My dad always has to be the first on his road. Only *I'm* the one who has to do the mowing." He scratched his head, frowning. "And, then, Dad says since we mowed so early in the season, we have to rake. Only *I'm* the one who does the raking. I'm totally wrecked!"

"So you don't want to go riding?" I asked, unable to conceal my disappointment.

He laughed. "No. I *need* to go riding. Just as long as we don't ride on *grass!*"

My mum came by, carrying one of the still-unpacked boxes from the back. I introduced Louis to her. She put down the box and shook his hand. I could tell by the look on her face that she was impressed with how good-looking he was.

A short while later, I pulled my new bike out of the garage and walked it over to Louis on the driveway.

It was a warm, sunny day with a few puffy clouds in the sky. The air was heavy and wet, almost like summer.

"Excellent bike!" Louis exclaimed, rubbing his hand along the shiny blue frame. "Really excellent!"

"You can't tell it's used, can you?" I asked. "It has one tiny scratch on the side here. That's all."

He admired the bike for a while longer.

"Excellent." He raised his eyes to mine. "Let's get going."

"Great," I said enthusiastically. I lifted my leg over the frame and straddled the bike, preparing to glide down the driveway. "Where shall we go?"

He narrowed his eyes in concentration. "Well. . ."

The sun disappeared behind one of the puffy clouds. A shadow rolled over us. The air immediately grew cooler.

I felt a sudden chill as Louis stared into my eyes and said, "Let's ride up to the falls."

# Eleven

Why did I feel that cold shiver of fear when Louis suggested we ride up to the falls?

I was angry at myself for feeling it.

I had no reason to be afraid of Louis. He seemed to really like me.

A horrible thing had happened up at the falls. But that was no reason to be frightened of Louis.

I reasoned that Louis was trying to get over Phoebe, trying to get over her death.

By returning to the falls with me, he was forcing himself to get on with his life. He was putting Phoebe behind him, putting all of the horror behind him.

That was my reasoning. I wished I had the courage to ask Louis if I was right. But I didn't feel I knew him well enough yet to bring it up.

He had never mentioned Phoebe to me.

I didn't think it was right for me to be the first to bring her up.

We rode in the middle of the street. There was hardly any traffic. Lawns were being mowed. And raked. Flowers were being planted. Gardens were being tended. Weeds were being pulled.

A group of little kids were gleefully climbing through the open walls of a new house being built. "This is *my* room!" a little boy cried. "No – that's the kitchen!" another boy corrected him.

"How are you doing?" Louis called back to me. He had got about three car-lengths ahead.

"Fine. I like this bike," I shouted.

"That's Jacob's house, remember?" Louis said, pointing to a square, white clapboard house with a ragged low hedge running along the front.

And just as Louis pointed, Jacob appeared on the gravel driveway. "Hey!" he called, spotting us immediately. "Where are you going?"

Louis wheeled around and pedalled onto the drive, his tyres sliding over the gravel as he hit the brakes. His front tyre came to a stop about a centimetre from Jacob who, grinning, raised both hands over his head in surrender.

I pulled up beside Louis and lowered both feet to the gravel.

"Hot day, huh?" Jacob said, grinning at me, pushing his

scraggly hair back off his forehead. The gold earring in his ear sparkled in the sunlight.

"Why don't we talk about the weather for a while," Louis said sarcastically. He gazed up at Jacob's house. Someone was watching us from the front window. Jacob's mum, I guess. "Did you get your bike fixed?" Louis asked.

"Pretty much," Jacob replied, grinning.

"Want to come with us?" Louis offered.

Jacob nodded. "I haven't had any better offers." He wiped his hands off on the legs of his jeans. "I'll get my bike. The tyres are low, but that's OK."

He started towards the back of the house, kicking up the gravel as he walked. After a few steps, he turned back. "Where are we riding?"

"Up to the falls," I answered.

"Huh?" Jacob's mouth dropped open. "What did you say?" His eyes were on Louis.

"Up to the falls," I repeated softly, surprised by Jacob's reaction.

Jacob continued to stare at Louis. "You sure?"

"Yeah. We're sure," Louis snapped. "Are you coming before suppertime or not? My bike is rusting, waiting for you."

"Hey, you're in a good mood," Jacob muttered. "Sure you want me to come along?"

"Get your bike," Louis instructed him.

Jacob disappeared round the back of the house. "Someone should mow Jacob's lawn," I said, gazing at the tall, overgrown grass and flourishing weeds.

"His parents won't trust him with a lawnmower," Louis replied, grinning. "They know he'd probably cut his foot off."

After a short while, Jacob came sailing down on a rickety old BMX bike, the seat raised up as high as it would go, both tyres nearly flat. "To the falls!" he cried, rolling past us, out of the driveway and into the street without slowing to look for cars.

"He's really messed up," Louis muttered to me, shaking his head.

Jacob was twirling his bike in tight circles, waiting for us, singing at the top of his lungs.

"He's your best friend," I said dryly.

"Why?" Louis asked, making a bewildered face.

Laughing, we followed Jacob into the street. We pedalled single file to town, which was crowded and busy, with cars actually double-parked on Main Street. Most people were going into the garden centre and the hardware store. Spring DIY time.

Past town, the road started to climb through the woods. Louis and I rode side by side behind Jacob, who zigzagged wildly from one side of the road to the other, riding no-hands most of the time.

After a bit, the road levelled out, and I could see a large red lorry coming towards us in the near distance.

"Hey, get over!" Louis called to Jacob. Jacob was riding no-hands on the wrong side of the road.

Staying in the wrong lane, Jacob turned back to us, a devilish grin on his face, his dark eyes glowing. "Watch what I do to this guy," he called.

"No way! Get over!" Louis screamed.

The red lorry seemed to grow larger and larger as it approached.

"Watch!" Jacob cried.

"Get over!" Louis screamed.

Jacob stayed on the wrong side, pedalling steadily, calmly, as if he had every right to be there, as if there wasn't a huge lorry barrelling right at him.

"This is stupid!" Louis screamed. His eyes were bugging out with fright.

The lorry honked its horn, a long, earthshaking diesel honk.

"Get over, idiot!" I could barely hear Louis's shout over the roar of the lorry's horn.

A wild grin on his face, Jacob just kept pedalling.

The lorry wasn't slowing down. It rumbled closer. Closer.

"Jacob – please!"

I closed my eyes as the blaring horn became an angry, deafening scream.

# Twelve

The ground seemed to shake.

I felt a powerful rush of hot air, which nearly blew me over.

When I opened my eyes, I saw Jacob seated on his bike, both feet on the ground on the other side of the road. He grinned at Louis and me and raised his fists triumphantly, cheering loudly for himself.

Louis tossed down his bike and angrily strode across the road to Jacob. I could hear the lorry rumbling away from us. It still felt to me as if the ground were shaking.

My heart was thudding in my chest. I felt dizzy. Straddling my bike, I stared across the road at Jacob as if he were a mirage.

"You could've been killed, man!" Louis screamed angrily at him.

"No way," Jacob insisted, his arms crossed over his chest,

his face bearing its usual goofy grin. "I've got timing."

"Timing? You're crazy!" Louis insisted.

"It's all timing," Jacob bragged, ignoring Louis's anger. Jacob turned his eyes to me. "Did you see the look on that lorry driver's face?"

"No, I didn't see anything," I admitted, "I closed my eyes." My legs were all trembly. My mouth was dry.

"I thought his face was going to explode!" Jacob laughed.

"That was really stupid," Louis said, scowling.

"I didn't get hit, did I?" Jacob demanded. "If I got hit, *that* would be stupid. If I'm lying here as flat as a pancake, then *that's* stupid. But I've got the timing down to an art. You know that, Louis."

Louis glared angrily at Jacob. He leaned close to his friend and lowered his voice. But I heard what he said anyway. He told Jacob, "You're just showing off for Abbie."

"Huh? Who – me?" Jacob glanced over Louis's shoulder at me. "No way, Louis."

Louis tossed up his hands, as if conceding defeat. "Are we going to ride or not?"

"Yeah. Sure. Let's go," Jacob replied, sounding hurt.

Louis walked quickly across the road, picked up his bike, and climbed onto it without looking at me. I could see that his mood had changed. Jacob's game of chicken with the lorry had really upset him.

"He could have bought it that time," Louis muttered, more to himself than to me.

We started to pedal, slowly picking up speed as the road curved through the woods, climbing towards the falls.

"Why does Jacob like to play such dangerous games?" I asked.

"Because I'm a dangerous guy!" Jacob exclaimed, overhearing me. He laughed gleefully. "I'm so *dangerous*!"

Louis just scowled.

A few minutes later, we turned off the road onto the bike path that led up to the top of the falls.

The falls were more beautiful than I'd remembered, the water sparkling like silver under the sun as it washed straight down from the cliff-edge.

"It smells so fresh and clean up here," I said, closing my eyes and taking a deep breath.

We left our bikes on the cycle path. I turned away from the falls to look at the woods. The leaves were all opening. The woods were so much brighter and greener than the week before.

I hoped that the beautiful scenery would help return Louis's good spirits. But when I turned back to the falls, I was startled to see that he had stepped right to the edge and was peering down, a grim expression on his face.

That's just where he'd stood when I first met him, I realized, feeling a sudden wave of dread sweep over my body.

That's just where he stood. On the very edge. Staring down so sadly.

I had thought then that Louis was going to jump.

I could feel my face grow hot, remembering that.

I suddenly became aware that Jacob had moved beside me. He was staring at Louis, too.

"I knew we shouldn't have come up here," Jacob said to me in a low voice, keeping his eyes on Louis. "I knew he wasn't ready to come up here yet."

"He was in a really good mood before," I said, feeling the cold spray off the falls on my face.

"Now he's not," Jacob said sharply, shaking his head. "We shouldn't be here."

He moved away from me and headed towards Louis, stopping a few feet from the edge. "Hey, Louis. . . ?"

Louis didn't turn round. He stood motionless, staring straight down into the streaming rush of white water.

"Louis, let's go," Jacob insisted, reaching out a hand as if intending to pull Louis away.

No reaction.

"Louis, let's go – OK?"

I took a few steps closer, suddenly very worried about Louis.

What was he thinking about?

What was he looking for?

Why wouldn't he answer Jacob?

Why wouldn't he step back from the cliff-edge?

I stepped up beside Jacob, who looked really worried. I think it was the first time I had seen Jacob with a serious expression on his face.

"Louis. . ." he called. "Earth calling Louis."

"Just a second," Louis said, not turning round.

"Come on, man," Jacob urged.

"Just a second," Louis repeated. "That's all it takes. A second. A split second. And then you're dead. Gone forever."

Jacob glanced at me, his features tight with worry. Then he grabbed Louis by the shoulder and pulled him back.

"Hey, what's the problem? Let go!" Louis protested.

"You're scaring us, man," Jacob told him, not letting go. He was pulling Louis back from the cliff-edge with both hands.

The spray drenched my face and hair. I suddenly felt cold, despite the bright sun overhead.

"I'm fine," Louis insisted.

"I don't like to hear you talking like that," Jacob said.

"Let's keep riding," I suggested, trying to sound cheerful.

"Yeah. Good idea," Jacob said.

I turned towards the cycle path and screamed. "Hey!"

Someone was back there, messing with my bike.

"Hey – get away!" I screamed.

Brushing the spray from my eyes, I began running to my bike.

The intruder had picked my bike up off the ground and was doing something to the handlebars.

I had only gone a few steps when I recognized who it was. Courtney!

# Thirteen

"Hey – get away!"

My trainers pounded the ground, kicking up dust as I ran towards Courtney. I could hear Louis and Jacob running behind me.

"Huh?" Courtney stood holding my bike by the handlebars, staring at me open-mouthed, her red hair dishevelled, gleaming in the bright sunlight.

I pulled up in front of her, gasping for breath. "What are you doing to my bike?" I demanded angrily.

"I'm just *looking* at it," she snapped back. "It's a lot like my cousin's bike."

I glared at her angrily, trying to catch my breath.

"I wasn't going to steal it or anything," she said, turning her snub nose up.

"What's the problem?" Jacob asked, running up beside me.

"Abbie thought I was going to run away with her bike," Courtney told him, frowning. "I just wanted to look at it. Here." She pushed the bike towards me.

I grabbed the frame and the seat to keep it from toppling over. "Courtney, I'm sorry. . ." I started.

"I'm not a thief, you know," Courtney said nastily.

"Hey, Abbie didn't mean it," Jacob said, trying to be helpful.

"Remember? Someone slashed my tyres last week," I told Courtney. "That's why I thought—"

"Well, it wasn't me!" Courtney interrupted.

I felt really embarrassed. I'd come running after Courtney like a crazy person, screaming at her, accusing her. And she was just looking at the bike.

"I'm really sorry," I said sincerely. "Really. I didn't mean. . ."

"OK, OK," Courtney said impatiently. Her bike was lying on its side a few feet down the cycle path. She picked it up and walked it back towards the tall granite rocks.

I wheeled mine after her, and Jacob followed.

"Where's Emily?" Courtney asked, shielding her eyes from the sun with one hand as her eyes followed the curve of the sloping bike path.

"Is Emily with you?" Jacob asked, following Courtney's gaze.

"Here she comes," Courtney announced.

I saw Emily, standing up as she pedalled, moving slowly up the hill. A few seconds later, she hopped off her bike and walked it up to us. She was red-faced and out of breath. Her dark hair was wet, a large strand matted against her perspiring forehead.

"Wow. I'm a little out of shape," she exclaimed breathlessly. "I've *got* to lose some weight."

"You look fine," Jacob said gallantly. He laughed. "You just need a better bike. Yours is too heavy. You should get one like Abbie's."

"But don't touch Abbie's, whatever you do," Courtney warned sarcastically, flashing me a dirty look. "If you touch her bike, she freaks."

"Huh?" Emily gazed at me, puzzled.

I leaned back against the rocks. "I made a mistake," I muttered. "I didn't mean. . ."

"Did you get that bike new or used?" Courtney asked.

"Used," I told her.

"It looks brand new," she said.

"It was such a pretty day," Emily said, pushing the hair off her forehead. "I told Courtney we should ride up. I was hoping you'd still be here."

"It's cooler up here," Courtney said.

"We should keep riding," Jacob suggested. "Keep going to Glenview, maybe."

"I want to cool off a bit first," Emily said, leaning her bike against the rocks.

"You know, we should start a bike club," Jacob said with great enthusiasm.

"Huh?" Emily narrowed her eyes at him.

"Yeah. A bike club," he repeated, undiscouraged. "We're just about the only ones in Shocklin Falls who like to ride around everywhere on our bikes, right?"

"Give me a break, Jacob," Emily said, rolling her eyes. "You ride that beat-up bike of yours because you can't afford a car, and your parents won't trust you with theirs."

"Smart parents," Courtney muttered, grinning.

"Hey, no way," Jacob protested. "I'm really into bikes, you know."

Emily made a sarcastic face.

"I'm just saying we could get together every weekend or something and maybe ride all over the place. You know, plan different routes. Bring food and stuff."

"I like the food part," I said, starting to feel hungry. I hadn't had much of a lunch.

"Forget it," Emily told Jacob. "I *hate* riding with you. You're too crazy. Always showing off. Trying to get yourself killed."

"Who? *Me?*" Jacob protested, grinning.

He had somehow conveniently forgotten about his little game of chicken with the lorry a short while before.

"Hey, where's Louis?" Courtney asked suddenly. "Isn't he up here with you?"

Louis.

I was so worked up about Courtney and my bike, I had forgotten all about Louis!

"He was with you," I told Jacob.

"No," Jacob replied. "I don't think so."

We all turned towards the falls.

No one there.

The water roared down, a fine white spray rising from the cliff-edge.

"Louis!" I called. "Louis, where are you?"

No reply.

I turned towards the woods. No sign of him.

When I turned back, Jacob was running to the cliff-edge, a frightened expression on his face.

Emily and Courtney were staring at me. "Where *is* he?" Courtney demanded, as if I were hiding him.

A wave of dread swept over me. Heavy fear, weighing me down, making it hard to breathe.

I raised my eyes to Jacob, standing at the cliff-edge over the falls.

The exact spot where Louis had been standing.

Jacob peered straight down, his features twisted in fear. "Did he jump?" he cried. "Did Louis jump?"

Behind me, Courtney uttered a high-pitched scream of horror.

# Fourteen

"No! No!" I heard a frightened voice shriek.

It took me a while to realize it was *me*!

Jacob took a step back from the falls. "I don't see anything down there," he called, cupping his hands over his mouth to be heard over the roaring waterfall.

"Look!" Courtney cried.

We turned to the cycle path.

There was Louis. On his bike. Dust flew up on both sides of his bike as he pedalled furiously away.

The four of us stood frozen in silence, staring after him, watching him disappear into the trees.

He never looked back.

When he vanished from view, I let out a long sigh of relief and dropped to my knees onto the ground.

At least Louis hadn't jumped.

I raised my eyes to Courtney and Emily. Emily had tears

in her eyes. Her shoulders were trembling. "I – I was so scared!" she stammered.

Courtney put a hand on Emily's shoulder to calm her.

"I mean, first Phoebe. Then. . ." Emily's voice trailed off

Jacob made his way back to us, his hands shoved into his jeans pockets, his head lowered.

"Why did he do that?" I asked him, my heart still pounding. "Why did Louis run away like that?"

Jacob shrugged grimly. "Beats me."

"I really thought he'd jumped," Courtney said in a quivering voice.

"Do you think he's *angry* with us for some reason?" Emily wondered. She leaned back against the rocks and pushed her damp hair off her face. She looked very pale, very upset.

"I *knew* we shouldn't have come up here," Jacob said heatedly. "It was too soon for Louis."

"But he had already come up here," I told Jacob. "Last week. I. . ."

"Was it *your* idea?" Jacob demanded loudly, staring angrily at me.

I gasped.

In that instant, I realized that Jacob didn't like me.

His outburst cut through me. I felt a stab of pain in my chest.

102

*He doesn't like me*, I thought, staring up at him, studying his angry expression.

"No. It wasn't my idea," I replied coldly, turning away from him.

"Well, it was a bad idea," Jacob insisted. "Don't you have any idea what Louis's been through?"

"Give her a break, Jacob," Emily said, coming to my defence. "Abbie knows the whole story."

"Let's get out of here," Courtney suggested, pushing away from the rocks and reaching for her bike. "Let's ride somewhere else, OK? This place gives me the creeps. I keep picturing Phoebe standing there."

"Yeah. Let's keep riding," Emily quickly agreed.

"I – I think I'd better get home," I told them. "I'm so behind on my coursework. I threw away the notes I'd typed onto the disk. And then it was all erased. I'm practically starting all over again."

"You sure?" Emily asked, pulling up her bike. "It's too nice out to be stuck inside doing schoolwork."

"I know," I sighed. "But I'd better do it."

"Don't be upset about Louis," Emily said as I retrieved my bike. "He's moody." She chuckled. "I guess you've noticed."

I said goodbye to them and headed down the hill, pedalling hard.

I *am* upset about Louis, I thought unhappily.

I'm *very* upset.

I thought this was a date. Why did he ride away and leave me there without saying a word?

Why did he do it?

That night, I had a frightening nightmare.

The dream was in black and white. Somehow the darkness of it, the sombre grey shadows, made it all the more horrifying.

In the dream, I was standing at the falls.

The water rushed down silently.

The whole dream was silent. Not a sound. Not a voice.

I stared at the rushing water, watched it plunge to the dark rocks below without making a splash.

It was cold up there. A wet chill fell over me, over everything. The sky was a cold charcoal-grey, a dead grey.

Someone stood at the edge of the cliff. Someone dressed in black.

I stared at her and listened to the silence.

Mist rose up from the plunging waters, grey and cold.

Even with her back turned to me, I realized it was Phoebe.

I called to her, but no sound came out of my mouth.

She turned round slowly.

I stared at her face.

I uttered a silent scream.

Her skin was gone. Her beautiful, wavy hair rested on top of a grinning skeleton.

Empty eye sockets stared at me blindly.

Her jawbone lowered, revealing a mouth full of perfect white teeth.

She turned quickly away from me.

Once again, she resumed her stance at the edge of the falls.

The water continued to sweep down in total silence.

The sky darkened. Shadows rolled over the hard, grey ground.

I crept up silently behind Phoebe.

Closer. Closer still.

I knew what I was going to do.

I raised my hands.

I was going to shove her over the edge.

Hands ready, I took another step. Another.

Suddenly, my voice returned. I spoke.

"I'm Louis's new girlfriend," I said as I prepared to push Phoebe. "I'm Louis's girlfriend now."

I said the words in a flat monotone, without any emotion at all.

The water flowed down, down, down. Silently.

I reached forward. I started to push her.

But as my hands lowered to her back, we suddenly changed places.

To my horror, I realized that I was now dressed in black.

I was now standing at the very edge of the silent falls.

"I'm Louis's new girlfriend," I said. "I'm Louis's dead girlfriend."

Was Phoebe behind me now?

Was Louis?

I couldn't turn round. I could only look down.

I knew that I was about to go over the edge, into the silently plunging waters.

I knew that I was about to die.

Silently. So silently.

Into the grey churning shadows below.

The ringing of the phone by my bed woke me up.

I sat up, startled, wide awake.

The dream faded slowly. The grey shadows lingered.

I blinked. Once. Twice.

The phone continued to ring.

I reached for it, then hesitated.

The cold fear I felt – was it from the dream? Or from the ringing of the phone?

Should I answer it?

Reluctantly, I lifted the receiver to my ear.

"It's me," said a dry, whispered voice.

# Fifteen

My breath caught in my throat.

I shut my eyes.

"Abbie?" the voice whispered. "Is that you?"

I swallowed hard.

"It's me. Louis," the voice whispered.

"Huh?" I cried. "Louis?"

"Who'd you *think* it was?" he asked, still whispering.

"What time is it?" I asked, squinting through the darkness at my clock radio. "Louis, it's nearly two."

"Oh. Sorry."

"Why are you whispering like that?" I demanded, my heart slowing to a normal pace.

"I don't want my parents to hear," he replied. "They'll take away my phone if they hear me calling so late."

"You scared me," I admitted. "I thought – I thought you were someone else."

"I just called to apologize," Louis said. "You know. For this afternoon."

"OK. Go ahead," I said. "Apologize."

"I apologize," he said earnestly.

I chuckled. "Apology accepted," I told him. "You could've called earlier, you know."

"I wanted to, but I had to go somewhere with my dad. Listen, Abbie, I shouldn't have run off like that. But . . . well . . . it's hard to explain."

"That's OK," I said, hearing how hard this was for him.

I was so relieved that he wasn't angry with me, that he didn't blame me for some reason.

"I shouldn't have suggested that we go up there," he continued. "I mean, it was just too soon. You probably don't know about Phoebe—"

"Yes. I heard," I interrupted.

He was silent for a long moment. "Yeah. I guess everyone talks about it," he said finally, with some bitterness.

"Emily told me . . . about Phoebe," I said softly.

As I said it, the dream washed over me. Again I saw the silent falls, the shifting grey shadows, the girl dressed in black, standing on the very edge, about to fall.

Was it Phoebe – or was it me?

"D'you want to get together tomorrow?" Louis asked, abruptly changing the subject. "We could go and see a film or something."

"I wish I could," I replied.

"I won't run away. Promise!" he quickly added.

"I've got to work on my research," I said. "I'll never get that coursework done at this rate."

"Oh. I see." He sounded very disappointed.

"Sorry," I said, and then I yawned loudly.

"Guess I'd better hang up," he whispered.

"I'm glad you called," I said honestly.

We said goodnight and hung up.

I lowered my head to the pillow and pulled up the duvet.

When I closed my eyes, images from my frightening dream returned, as if they'd been waiting for me.

No, I thought, opening my eyes wide, trying to drive the pictures away. No, I don't want to think about Phoebe now. I don't want to think about this.

"Louis didn't push Phoebe," I whispered to myself, staring up at the dark ceiling. "Louis didn't push her. I *know* he didn't!"

I had just got down to work the next afternoon, papers and books spread out all over the dining room table, when the doorbell rang. Since I was the only one at home, I ran to answer it.

"Emily!" I cried out in surprise.

She smiled at me. She was wearing a blue jumper over white tennis shorts. Her hair was tied loosely behind her head.

"I really have to work," I told her, holding open the screen door. "I don't have time to. . ."

"I know," she said, stepping past me into the front hallway. "I brought you a bunch of books." She lowered her shoulder so I could see the bulging bag on her back. "You know. For research."

"Hey, thanks," I cried, genuinely grateful. "That's really nice of you. The library is closed on Sundays, so. . ."

"I think it's all stuff you can use," she said, groaning as she pulled the bag off.

I led her into the dining room, and she emptied the contents of the bag onto the table. "I'll only stay for a minute," she said, pulling out a chair and sitting down. "Have you talked to Louis?"

I told her about his late-night apology.

"Weird," she said. And, then, fiddling with her hair, she added, "Poor guy." Her expression changed to anger. "I've just about *had* it with Jacob."

"Huh? What do you mean?" I asked, sifting through the books she had brought, glancing at the titles.

"He's just impossible," Emily complained, frowning. "He's

such a dork. He can never be serious. We went to the cinema last night, and he called out funny remarks through the whole film. The people around us were really angry. They didn't think he was funny at all. I thought they were going to punch his lights out."

I tsk-tsked, only half concentrating on what Emily was saying. I really did want to get back to work.

"Jacob's parents actually let him take the car last night," Emily continued, sighing unhappily. "They haven't let him drive it in weeks. So what did he do? He drove it into a ditch, and we had to be towed. *Aaaaagh!*" She uttered a cry of total frustration, pounding both fists on the table.

"What a drag," I said, trying to sound sympathetic. "Jacob really is a crazy guy."

"I'm going to make a change," Emily said, locking her eyes on mine. I had the feeling that she had made up her mind just that second. "I'm going to break up with him. I really am. I don't know why I've put up with him for so long."

She got to her feet and picked up her empty bag. She started to the doorway, then stopped. "Don't say anything, Abbie. To Jacob, I mean. Or to anyone."

"OK," I agreed.

"In case I chicken out or change my mind," Emily said.

I suppose I should have said something nice about Jacob. Maybe that's what Emily wanted. Maybe she was confiding in me so that I'd defend Jacob and make her change her mind about breaking up with him.

But I remembered Jacob's angry outburst, the way he shouted at me up at the falls. I remembered the intense look of dislike on his face as he glared at me.

And I guess I had decided that I didn't like Jacob, either.

So I didn't defend him.

Emily left, determined to break up with him. Before the screen door had slammed behind her, I had buried myself in my research books.

I worked for a couple of hours, but my mind kept wandering. The hideous dream wouldn't fade away. It kept invading my thoughts. And I found myself daydreaming about Louis, making up conversations with him in my mind.

My thoughts wandered to Phoebe. I wondered what she was like, what her voice sounded like, what her laugh was like.

I glanced up at the clock. It was a little past four, and I hadn't covered much ground at all with my research.

I stood up and stretched, feeling restless.

I couldn't sit there any more. I had to get out, get some exercise. I had to clear my mind.

I pulled a long-sleeved shirt over my T-shirt and hurried outside to get my bike out of the garage. It was a grey, overcast day. Heavy, dark clouds hovered menacingly low. I could hear the rumble of thunder in the distance.

But I didn't care. I had to ride for a while. Maybe a long while.

As I pedalled down the drive and into the street, the cool, damp air felt good against my hot cheeks. The wind brushed my hair back as I stood up and pedalled harder, picking up speed.

Faster. Faster.

I wanted to ride faster than my thoughts. I wanted to ride away from the frightening dream, from Phoebe's smiling face – from everything and everyone.

Houses and lawns rolled past in a grey-green blur. A little kid in a yellow raincoat waved to me from his driveway, and I waved back but didn't slow my pace.

Faster. Faster.

My heart was pounding. I could feel the blood pulsing at my temples.

There were cold drops of rain in the air. The sky grew even darker.

I rode past the college where my parents worked, then turned onto a path that led round the back. The path ended behind the car-park, dark and empty.

The distant thunder had become a steady rumble, moving closer. I headed my bike towards the woods behind the college.

I hadn't had a chance to explore these woods. Someone had told me they stretched on forever.

The tall trees with their freshly unfurled leaves blocked out most of the remaining light. I felt a sudden flash of fear as I realized it was nearly as dark as night here.

But I couldn't stop riding. I wasn't ready to turn round. It felt so good to be speeding through the cold air, under the dark trees.

At first, the only sounds were the whisper of the trees, the low rumble of thunder, and the scud of my bike tyres along the curving path.

But then I heard another sound.

Behind me.

Close behind me.

I turned and saw someone on the path. Someone dressed in dark clothes.

Running.

Running after me.

My dream suddenly flashed into my mind. All black and white.

Black and white like the figure chasing me.

Panic gripped my legs.

I wanted to speed up, to get away from the dark dream.

He was closing the gap, running at full speed, his shoes slapping the ground noisily.

"Ohh!"

I cried out as my front tyre hit something in the path. A rock, probably.

I didn't have time to see it.

The bike flew out of control.

I saw the trees tilt. Then the ground came up to meet me.

I landed hard on my side with a jolt of pain that ran up and down my entire body.

The bike fell on top of me, the front tyre spinning rapidly.

*He's got me*, I thought.

# Sixteen

y heart thudding in my chest, I tried frantically to push the bike off me.

I heard my pursuer's footsteps stop. He was standing over me.

I glanced up.

"Ryan!" I cried

Breathing hard, he bent down, grabbed the handlebars, and pulled the bike away.

He leaned it against a tree, then wiped the sweat off his forehead with the sleeve of his black hoody.

"Ryan – what are you *doing* here?" I demanded in a high-pitched, shrill voice I barely recognized.

He took my arm and helped me up. "Are you OK?" he asked, ignoring my question. "Are you hurt?"

"No, I don't think so," I replied shakily. I tried to brush the mud off the leg of my jeans.

It started to rain. First I heard the *tap-tap-tap* of raindrops on the leaves overhead. Then I felt large, cold drops on my hair.

"Why did you race off like that?" Ryan asked, staring at me, a bewildered expression on his slender face.

"I – I don't know," I admitted, embarrassed. "I thought you were. . ."

*Someone from my dream?*

What *did* I think?

Why *did* I panic like that?

"I thought I was alone," I explained. "When I saw someone chasing me. . ."

"Didn't you hear me calling you?" he asked. He pulled a leafy twig off the sleeve of my shirt.

The pattering of raindrops against the leaves grew louder. I could feel the rain on my shoulders now. "We're going to get soaked," I said. I picked up my bike and examined it. It seemed OK. It wasn't bent or anything. "I think I hit a rock."

"Yeah," Ryan agreed. He pointed to the path. A square-shaped stone jutted up right in the middle. "You were really moving!" Ryan exclaimed, still studying my face intently.

"Yeah," I said, starting to catch my breath. "So what were you doing here?"

I began walking my bike back towards the college. Ryan followed, walking close beside me.

"Phoebe and I used to walk here all the time," he told me, turning his eyes to the trees up ahead. "This was where we used to hang out."

I waited for him to continue, but he didn't. We walked on in silence for a while.

The rain was cold but gentle. The trees shook as if shivering. My hair was soaked, but it felt refreshing. Cleansing, somehow.

"Phoebe was such a good friend," Ryan said, breaking the silence. His expression was thoughtful. His narrow shoulders were hunched under his hoody as he trudged along beside me, hands shoved in his pockets. He avoided my eyes.

I think he expected me to reply, but I didn't know what to say.

"We used to talk about everything," he went on. "She told me things she'd *never* tell Louis." A strange smile formed on Ryan's face. He kept his eyes straight ahead.

I wondered if what he'd said was true.

Why was he telling me this now?

I barely knew him. I'd only talked to him once. Why was he confiding in me?

He seems terribly lonely, I realized.

"She was my best friend," he said softly. He stopped suddenly. He grabbed my shoulder, forcing me to stop. I nearly dropped my bike.

118

Ryan turned his eyes to mine in an intense stare. "I want *you* to be my friend, too," he said with emotion.

"W-well. . ." I stammered. He was squeezing my arm so hard, it hurt. "Ryan, I. . ."

"I want you to be my good friend, too."

Still squeezing my shoulder, he pressed his face against mine and tried to kiss me.

I was so startled!

My breath caught in my throat.

His lips felt hot and dry against mine. He pressed them against me too hard, too desperately.

He was really hurting me.

With a bit of a struggle, I shoved him away. "Ryan – stop!"

He looked surprised for a moment, then hurt.

I felt terribly confused. And frightened.

He was so violent. So needy.

I jumped on my bike and started to pedal, standing up. "Bye," I shouted, without turning back.

The rain flew into my face, coming down heavier now. Thunder roared nearby, seeming to shake the dark trees.

"You'll be sorry if you hang around with Louis!" I heard Ryan shout. "You'll be sorry!"

I turned back to make sure he wasn't chasing after me.

Thunder roared.

"Poor Phoebe!" Ryan shouted as it echoed through the trees. "She was sorry. I tried to warn her!"

He shouted something else, but it was drowned out by thunder.

I was too far away to hear him now. The back of the college came into view with a flash of bright white lightning.

I pedalled faster, soaked to the skin.

"Ryan's crazy," I said into the wind, his voice still lingering in my ears. "Ryan's really crazy."

After school on Monday, I was on my way to the computer room. It was going to be my hangout for the rest of the week. I was determined to get all my research notes typed in so that I could organize them and then start writing my paper.

If only we had a decent computer at home, I thought.

My birthday was only a week away. But with all the expense of moving into a new house, I knew my parents wouldn't buy me a computer.

As I hurried down the hallway, kids were pulling out their school bags, slamming their lockers shut, and heading out of the building.

I saw Courtney speeding off in the other direction, her red hair dishevelled, an intense, thoughtful expression on her face. "Hey, Courtney!" I called to her as she passed.

But she didn't seem to hear me. She kept right on going.

What's *her* problem? I wondered.

For a brief moment, I suspected that she had deliberately ignored me. But I decided that couldn't be true.

"Hey, Abbie, wait!" a familiar voice called. I saw Emily waving to me from behind a group of laughing kids who were blocking the hallway.

"Hi, Emily. How's it going?" I asked when she finally managed to get over to me. She had her hair up high on her head in a new style. She was wearing a white top tucked into a very short, green-and-white skirt.

"Listen, the cheerleaders are having a cake sale in the gym," she said breathlessly, staring at the stack of books in my arms. "Courtney and I are meeting down there. D'you want to join us?"

"I'd really like to," I said, sighing. "But I can't, Emily. I've really got to get these notes done. I'm going to be staying late every afternoon."

Emily made a face.

"No. Really!" I insisted. "I'm so far behind. Especially since my disk was erased."

Emily waved to someone down the corridor. Then she turned back to me. "Why don't you type really fast, then hurry down to the gym?"

"No. No way," I told her.

"OK. Call you later," she said, giving me a little wave, then

121

turning and hurrying down the hallway.

I trudged into the computer room, lugging my armload of books.

Miss Elwood, the ICT teacher, was at her desk in the back of the room, studying a thick software catalogue. She glanced up as I entered, smiled, and returned to her book.

There were a couple of other kids I didn't recognize, typing away at keyboards, their faces illuminated in green from the glow of their monitor screens.

I put down the stack of books beside the computer I always used. It wasn't one of the new Macs, but I really liked the keyboard. No one else seemed to like this computer, so it was always free, ready for me to use.

I really enjoyed doing research. I found it strangely satisfying – digging up little bits of information, then putting them in some kind of order. It was sort of like a puzzle. And it was fun to see the pieces come together.

I turned on the power, and the computer hummed to life.

I got my disk from the disk file, and I lowered my fingers to the keyboard.

I felt the first painful jolt as my fingers pressed the keys.

Bright light – like lightning – shot over my hands, with a loud crackle.

I heard a buzz.

Felt another jolt of pain.

Electricity crackled over my hands. Shot through my body.

Gasping, I tried to pull my hands away.

But the crackling blue-white current held me prisoner.

"H-h-h-h—" I tried to call for help. But the current was forcing my entire body to tremble out of control. "H-h-h-h—"

Out of control. . .

The crackling grew louder. The blue-white light snapped around me.

It grew brighter. Brighter.

The pain was so intense!

Then everything went black.

# Seventeen

A thin blue light trailed through the utter blackness.
The light glowed brighter. Brighter.

Cold blue light, ribbon-thin.

It exploded into a wash of bright colours.

I opened my eyes.

Miss Elwood's worried face came into sharp focus.

Everything seemed so bright, so clear. As if all the lights had been turned up. As if the white electricity had given everyone a brighter-than-daylight glow.

"She's opening her eyes," Miss Elwood told someone else in the room.

I slowly realized that I was no longer sitting at the computer. Staring up at the ceiling lights above Miss Elwood's frowning face, I saw that I was flat on my back on the floor.

Everything seemed to be vibrating. Pulsing. Buzzing.

"Miss Elwood?"

My voice came out flat, nearly a whisper.

"She's talking," Miss Elwood told someone near the door. I heard shuffling feet, murmurs, muffled voices.

Miss Elwood peered down at me, her face just a few inches above mine. "Abbie, can you hear me?" she asked anxiously.

"Yes." Again, my voice didn't sound like me.

"Can you see me?" Miss Elwood demanded, so close I could smell peppermint on her breath.

"Yes," I told her.

I tried to sit up. But I felt dizzy, so I dropped back down.

Why was everything vibrating like that?

I thought I heard the crackling sound. The crackling of electricity. But it was only in my mind.

I turned my head and saw several other kids and a few teachers huddled against the wall.

"What happened?" I asked.

"You got a bad shock," Miss Elwood said.

"Huh?" I stared up at her. She pulled her head back a little. I felt a little stronger. I sat up.

The lights were dimming to normal. The crackling stopped.

"You got a bad shock. From the computer." She pointed. The old computer had been unplugged, the wire draped over the monitor.

"Those machines aren't supposed to do that," Miss Elwood said.

*Right*, I thought bitterly. *That's pretty obvious, isn't it!*

"The electricity just shot out from the keyboard," Miss Elwood explained.

I got to my feet. I felt strange. Not weak or dizzy.

I felt *crazy*. Really *pumped*.

I felt like running for ten miles. Or putting my fist right through the wall.

It was from all that electricity, I guess.

"Did you touch the plug or something?" Miss Elwood demanded, biting her lower lip.

"Uh-uh," I said. "Only the keyboard."

"I can't understand it," she said, staring at me intently.

*I can*, I thought.

*I can understand it.*

The anger surged in my chest like a jolt of electricity.

I saw the white light again.

My anger raged through me like a powerful current.

Courtney!

Courtney had tampered with the computer.

I knew it in a burst of angry white light.

That's why Courtney was running down the hall with that wild look on her face.

That's why Courtney ran right past me without seeing

me, without stopping.

Courtney had wired the keyboard.

She took that electrical class on Saturdays. That's where she learned how.

And now she had tried to kill me with electricity.

She had tried to kill me to keep me away from Louis. To make her threats come true.

She had wired the keyboard. To kill me.

Kill me. Kill me. Kill me.

"Abbie – come back!" Miss Elwood shouted.

I didn't even realize that I was running until I reached the hallway.

"Come back!" I could hear her scream.

But I kept running. I couldn't stop myself.

I couldn't stop my rage.

It raced through my body like a powerful jolt of current.

I heard the hideous crackling sound again. I saw the eerie blue light. It filled my eyes, shimmering brighter and brighter as I ran – until it suddenly burst into the brightest, angriest red, so red, so angry; I shut my eyes.

*Courtney did it*, I told myself.

Her name repeated in my mind until it became an ugly word.

Where was I running?

I'm not sure I knew.

The anger was driving me forward. The red electric anger was moving me blindly through the halls, past rows of lockers, past doorways, all red, all blazing red.

When I burst into the crowded gym, I wasn't sure where I was. Faces came into focus, bright focus. I saw smiling faces. I saw cheerleaders in their uniforms. I saw kids milling about the tables of the cake sale.

I'm here, I told myself. My anger, my *fury*, had brought me here.

To do what?

And then I saw Emily and Courtney against the tile wall. And standing next to Courtney was Louis.

She had one hand on the shoulder of his jumper.

They were laughing.

Their laughter, the hand on his shoulder, her dishevelled red hair – it was all too much.

With an angry shriek that I didn't even realize had come from me, I lunged across the gym. Ignoring the startled cries around me, I threw myself on Courtney.

Her eyes bugged out in shock as I wrapped my hands around her throat.

I leaped at her with such force that we both toppled to the floor.

As the red light crackled and buzzed, I wrestled her down.

I heard screams. Loud cries. Alarmed voices.

Red. I saw only red.

Then I felt strong hands on my shoulders, pulling me up, pulling me away.

As the hands held me back, Courtney scrambled to her feet.

She was red-faced, as red as my anger, and her eyes were filled with tears.

I turned to see who had pulled me away. It was Emily.

"Just chill!" she was shouting in my ear. "Chill, Abbie! Just chill!"

Courtney stood hunched over in front of me, her hands pressed against her knees, panting loudly.

The gym buzzed and crackled with excited voices.

With a swift motion, I jerked myself free of Emily.

Courtney raised herself warily, glaring at me, her chest heaving.

"You tried to kill me!" I screamed at her.

Her face filled with surprise, but she didn't reply.

"But you're not going to scare me away! You're not!" I shrieked.

"Abbie, what's your problem?" Courtney snapped, rubbing her throat with one hand. "What is your *problem*?"

"You know what I'm talking about," I said through gritted teeth, lowering my voice as I saw two teachers approaching.

"No, I don't. I *don't!*" Courtney insisted. "You're messed up, Abbie. You really are!"

I opened my mouth to say something, but no sound came out. Angrily, helplessly, I turned to Louis. He stood staring at me, his hands balled up tensely at his sides.

"Well, say something!" I shouted at him. "Aren't you going to say *anything?*"

His face reddened. All expression seemed to disappear. He stared back at me, a stone face. "Abbie, I don't know what's going on," he said.

The teachers were making their way across the gym to see what the fuss was about.

"Louis. . ." I started. But I didn't know what to say, either.

My anger, I realized, had faded. The bright red current that had brought me storming into the gym had vanished, as if someone had pulled the plug.

Now, with everyone staring at me, with everyone talking about me, I felt embarrassed. Humiliated.

"You're messed up, Abbie," Courtney repeated. "I mean it. You're really messed up."

With a groan of defeat, I turned and ran.

I pushed my way through a group of gawking kids and kept running.

My chest heaving, my head throbbing, I shoved open the gym doors and raced through them.

I heard Emily calling me from the gym. But I never looked back.

I ran up the stairs, panting loudly, stumbling, as I climbed. Then I started down the front hall, my trainers thundering over the hard floor.

I turned into the corridor where my locker was. Some of the lights had been turned out. The hall looked like a dark, empty tunnel.

My loud gasps echoing against the tile walls, I stopped short when a figure stepped out of the darkness.

She moved silently towards me. And when her face came into the light, I uttered a silent gasp of horror.

It was Phoebe.

# Eighteen

I stood in the centre of the hall and stared at her, my eyes practically popping out of my head, my mouth wide open.

She stopped, too. Her blonde hair caught the light. She was very pale, paler than her photograph.

Pale as a ghost.

She wore a dark green jumper over brown shorts. She had a blue bag slung over one shoulder.

*Phoebe, what are you doing here?* I thought. *You're dead.*

I suddenly realized I'd forgotten to breathe. I exhaled with a loud whoosh.

"Are you OK?" she asked. Her pale forehead wrinkled in concern.

"I – I don't know," I stammered. I couldn't stop staring at her. I'd never seen a ghost before.

I took a step back, suddenly frightened.

"It's so dark in this hall with most of the lights out," she said. "Don't they usually leave them on?" She had a smooth, soft voice.

I didn't answer her. I just stared in disbelief. The photograph, the sad, sad photograph had come to life.

Phoebe had come back.

But how?

"I'm Natasha Powell," she said, shifting the bag to her other shoulder. "You're new here, right?"

"Huh?"

I was speechless. I couldn't seem to focus on anything. "What did you say your name was?" I managed to ask.

"Natasha," she repeated.

And then she gasped, and all the life seemed to drain from her face. "I'm not Phoebe," she said softly, so softly I could barely hear her. She took a few steps towards me, her pale blue eyes suddenly moist. "Is that what you thought? Did you think I was my sister?"

"They never told me she had a sister," I mumbled, still shaken.

"What?" She hadn't heard me. She gazed at me with concern. "Listen, are you feeling OK?"

"I'm sorry, Natasha," I said, shaking my head as if trying to clear it. "I'm having a really bad day."

"Tell me about it," she replied, rolling her eyes. "I just had to stay late to re-take a physics exam."

"I'm Abbie Kiernan," I said, starting to recover my wits. "I've just moved to Shocklin Falls, and. . ."

"You're Louis's new girlfriend," she said with an odd smile.

"I don't know," I told her. "I haven't really seen him that much. I. . ."

"D'you want to get a Coke or something?" she asked, starting towards the door. "Physics exams make me really thirsty. And this dark hall is giving me the creeps. It's like a tomb." She blushed, probably thinking about Phoebe.

"Yeah. Great," I said, following after her. "I'll be glad to get out of here, too."

Courtney flashed into my mind. Courtney, glaring angrily at me.

Had I made a fool of myself back in the gym? Or had Courtney really tried to electrocute me?

I tried not to think of it as I followed Natasha out of the building, into the sunlight of a warm spring afternoon. We walked to a small coffee shop a couple of streets towards town and slid into a booth near the back.

"I really want to apologize," I said, after we'd ordered Cokes and chips. "I mean, for the way I stared at you. You must've thought I was *nuts*!"

"Yeah, I did," Natasha said, smiling. Her eyes crinkled when she smiled, and a dimple appeared on her right cheek.

I wondered if Phoebe had the same dimple.

"I guess I freak a lot of kids out," she said softly, lowering her eyes to the tabletop. "Since I look so much like Phoebe. I'm a year and a half older than she was. But people were always mistaking us. I suppose you know what happened to Phoebe."

"Yeah. Some of it," I said awkwardly. "I mean Emily told me the story. I'm so sorry. Really."

"I feel so bad for Louis, and Courtney, too," Natasha said. The Cokes arrived, and she took a long sip from the straw.

"Courtney?" I asked, startled.

"Yeah. You know. The three of them went biking that day, the day Phoebe . . . died." She took another long sip, nearly emptying the glass.

"I didn't know Courtney went, too," I said, unable to conceal how stunned I was. "Emily never told me. . ."

"She was probably protecting Courtney," Natasha said. "You know Emily and Courtney have been friends since they were tiny."

"I'm sorry to be so nosy," I said, spinning my glass between my hands. "You don't have to answer if you don't want to. But –" I took a deep breath – "do you think that Louis or Courtney. . . ?"

I couldn't finish my question.

135

It was too horrible.

"Do I think they had anything to do with my sister's death?" she finished it for me. She closed her eyes, then shook her head. "No. Maybe. No."

"Natasha, you really don't have to answer," I said, putting my hand on her slender wrist.

"I don't know *what* to think!" she declared emotionally. "I've spent so many nights unable to go to sleep, just thinking and thinking about it."

She slurped up the rest of the Coke. The waitress brought the chips. Natasha asked for another Coke.

"Louis and Phoebe were always fighting," she confided to me. "Always. They were always breaking up, then making up. It was a really stormy relationship. But I really don't think Louis would *kill* her because of any stupid fight."

"And Courtney?" I asked.

"I think Courtney was jealous of Phoebe. I don't know. I don't know Courtney very well. I think Courtney probably liked Louis. A lot. But, come on, Abbie. People don't kill people over things like that."

"Someone tried to kill *me*," I blurted out.

"Huh?" She dropped the ketchup bottle. It clattered onto the tabletop, but didn't break.

I told her what had happened to me in the computer room.

Natasha frowned, wrinkling her pale forehead thoughtfully. "Those old computers," she muttered. "It probably shorted out. You have no proof that someone rigged it up."

I reluctantly agreed. I was instantly sorry that I'd told her about it. I mean, she had enough problems, enough sadness of her own. She didn't need to hear about my problems.

After that, we chatted for a short while, being careful not to talk about anything important. I liked her. She seemed like a really sweet, thoughtful girl. Even though she was so pale and slight, she seemed to have real strength, the strength to deal with all of the sadness she'd experienced.

We lived in different directions, so we said goodbye outside the coffee shop.

The sun was lowering itself in the late afternoon sky, a red ball sinking below the green trees. The air carried the chill of evening.

I gave Natasha a little wave, then stood watching her walk away. She was so light, she seemed to float away, like a pale ghost, disappearing into the cold, blue afternoon.

The ringing phone woke me up late that night.

Still half asleep, I lifted the receiver.

Again, a frightening, raspy voice whispered angrily in my ear:

"*Louis will kill you, too, if you don't stay away. Louis will kill you too.*"

Whoever it was hung up.

I was wide awake now.

I replaced the receiver.

As soon as I hung it up, the phone rang again.

My hand hovered over the receiver, trembling.

Should I pick it up?

# Nineteen

As my hand hesitated over the phone, something hit me hard in the stomach.

I uttered a silent gasp and leaped to my feet.

To my relief, it was only Goggles. I guess the phone had woken him.

The phone rang again. Goggles mewed and lowered himself onto my pillow.

I picked up the phone receiver. "Hello?"

"Hi, Abbie. It's me."

"Emily?" I read the time on my clock radio. It was nearly one.

"Did I wake you?"

"It's so late," I said, sitting down on the edge of the bed. I reached out a hand to pet Goggles, but he jumped off the bed.

"I'm sorry," Emily said, "but I've just been so upset. I've

been thinking about you and Courtney all night, Abbie. You know. What happened in the gym."

I shivered. The bedroom window was open. The breeze blowing in was really cold.

"Yeah. What about it?" I muttered, the whole angry scene flashing through my mind.

"Courtney was terribly hurt," Emily continued. "I've never seen her so hurt. And upset."

"Too bad," I said sarcastically.

"You really should apologize to her," Emily said.

My mouth dropped open. I was speechless at the suggestion.

"Abbie? Are you still there?"

"Apologize to Courtney?" I cried. "Emily, are you out of your mind? She tried to *kill* me!"

"Abbie, listen—"

"She wired the computer keyboard to *electrocute* me!" I screamed, forgetting that I might wake up the rest of the family.

"She couldn't have," Emily replied softly.

"Huh? What do you mean?"

"Courtney couldn't rig up anything like that."

"What about that electrical class you two are taking?" I demanded.

"We've only had two classes," Emily told me. "We don't

140

know anything. There's no way Courtney could wire up a computer. She can barely change a lightbulb."

"Then *who* did it?" I asked shrilly. I could feel myself going out of control. My throat tightened in anger. And in fear.

"How should I know?" Emily replied. "It was probably an accident, Abbie. But you shouldn't have blamed Courtney. She called me tonight. She couldn't stop crying."

"Boo-hoo," I said nastily. But I was beginning to feel guilty.

This afternoon, I had been so frightened and so angry, I didn't know *what* I was doing. When I ran into the gym, all I could see was bright red. I could've strangled Courtney then. I really wanted to harm her.

But maybe Emily was telling the truth. Maybe I blamed the wrong person.

"Why are you sticking up for Courtney?" I demanded, pulling the duvet over my bare legs.

"She's my friend," Emily said. "And she's really not a bad person, Abbie. I know you got off to a bad start with her. But Courtney is really OK."

"Well, how come you didn't tell me that Courtney was up at the falls when Phoebe died?"

That question caught Emily off-guard.

There was a long silence.

Finally, she answered, speaking slowly, carefully. "It was old news, Abbie. I didn't think you needed to know it. I didn't want to turn you against Courtney. I thought all three of us could be good friends."

She sighed. There was another long silence.

"I guess I should tell you the whole story," she said quietly. "Courtney had a thing about Louis for a while. I don't think Louis was ever seriously interested in her. He just saw her as a friend. But sometimes when he and Phoebe were fighting, he'd go out with Courtney. And that's all. After Phoebe died, it was all over between them."

"Oh, really?" I said, not intending it to come out so nastily. "Then how come Courtney and Louis went out together last weekend?"

"It wasn't a real date," Emily said. "Really. Courtney told me all about it. At the class on Saturday. It wasn't a date at all."

"Listen, Emily," I said impatiently, watching the curtains flutter in front of my open window. "Someone is trying really hard to frighten me away from Louis. And I think it's Courtney."

"I don't," Emily replied quickly. "I don't think it's Courtney. No way. For all I know, it could be Louis himself."

"Huh?" It was my turn to be caught off-guard.

"What are you *saying*, Emily?" I demanded, squeezing the phone cord tightly in my free hand. "Louis?"

"You don't know him very well," Emily replied. "Sometimes I think he's really crazy. Maybe even dangerous."

"Louis? Dangerous?"

"Maybe."

"Well, I don't know, Emily. He's really moody, but. . ." I didn't know what to say. "I *will* apologize to Courtney," I told Emily, changing the subject. "I guess I really owe her an apology. I'll invite her for Saturday night. To my birthday party. It's not really a party. Just sort of an open house. You and Jacob are coming, right?"

"Yeah," she replied. "I mean, I am. I don't know about Jacob. I might break up with him before Saturday. He's just too big a dork." She yawned. "But we've been through that before. I think I have to go to sleep now," she said, yawning again.

I said goodnight and we both hung up.

"Goggles? Are you here?" I called softly.

I had an urgent need to hug something.

But the bad cat had run from the room.

Everyone seemed to be having a good time at my birthday open house on Saturday night. Our living room isn't exactly enormous, but no one seemed to mind being jammed in like sardines.

The music was really loud, and the laughter was even louder.

I boiled up a huge pot of spaghetti. And everyone stood or sat around with their bowls of spaghetti, slurping it up as best they could. It was actually a very funny sight.

Emily showed up with Jacob. They seemed to be as together as always. I guessed Emily had changed her mind about breaking up with him during the week.

Courtney showed up, too. She even brought me a present. I could tell when I took it from her that it was a book.

I had called Courtney the morning after my conversation with Emily and apologized for twenty minutes, begging her forgiveness. I only did it because of Emily. I was still very suspicious of Courtney, in spite of Emily saying what a good person she was.

Louis seemed very relaxed. I could see he was having a good time, joking with some of his friends, laughing more than I'd ever seen him.

As I passed by him outside the kitchen, he grabbed both my hands and, smiling, started to pull me towards the corner of the living room where some kids were dancing. "Come on," he urged. "I really like this song. Come on. Let's dance."

I started to go with him, but I heard someone knocking on the back door. Louis got a pouty look on his face as I pulled away from him and headed through the kitchen to see who was at the back.

"Ryan!" I cried in surprise, pulling open the kitchen door and flicking on the back porchlight.

He looked terribly embarrassed. He fiddled with his glasses, avoiding my eyes. "I – I didn't know you were having a party," he stammered. "I just stopped by to . . . uh . . . say hi. See if you were busy, but. . ."

"Come in," I told him. "It's just an open house. For my birthday. Why don't you stay a while, have some spaghetti?" I pointed to the big, steaming pot on the stove.

I didn't really want Ryan at my party. Actually, he gave me the creeps.

But what could I do? There he was.

He came in, looking very reluctant. I hurried back to Louis in the living room.

"The song's over," Louis said, still pouting.

"I'll play it again," I said, moving to the CD player.

He grabbed my arm gently. "That's OK. Hey, want to go biking with me tomorrow afternoon? If it's a nice day?"

"Yeah. Sure. I guess," I replied.

Then he surprised me by wrapping his arms round my waist and lowering his face to mine in a really intense kiss.

I closed my eyes at first and returned the kiss.

When I opened them, I saw Courtney staring at us from across the room, an unhappy frown frozen on her face.

145

*What's her problem?* I asked myself silently.

Ignoring her, I kissed Louis again.

"What a mess!" my mother cried, her eyes surveying the kitchen.

"It's not as bad as it looks," I said. "It's *worse!*"

Mum and I both laughed.

"Maybe spaghetti wasn't such a great idea," she said, staring at a wide puddle of tomato sauce in the middle of the kitchen floor.

"It seemed like a good idea at the time," I sighed.

"I'll change my shoes. Then we'll get to work," Mum said, pushing a strand of blonde hair off her forehead.

"No. Really. You don't have to help," I told her. "You and Dad were so good tonight, hiding up in your room the whole night."

"We *were* good, weren't we?" Mum said, smiling. "But I'll come and help you clean up anyway, Abbie. Otherwise you'll be here all night."

She started towards the doorway, then stopped abruptly.

"Hey, you left the spaghetti water on," she said.

"No, I didn't," I insisted. "I turned it off. I remember."

"Well, it's boiling over," Mum said, irritated.

We both made a mad dash to the stove and turned off the burner. The lid was bouncing around on top of the pot, steaming liquid frothing up, running down the sides, onto the stove.

I lifted the lid. "Yuck. What's this white stuff?" I asked.

Bobbing on the top of the boiling water was a large white hunk of cotton.

"How did this get in here?" I asked, making a face. "What on earth is it?"

I poked it with a long wooden spoon.

As I rolled it over, two blank, blue eyes came into view.

When I finally realized what it was, I started to scream.

It wasn't a hunk of cotton bubbling at the top of the pot.

It was Goggles.

# Twenty

Louis showed up at my house the next afternoon. He came walking into the kitchen, wearing a black-and-red sleeveless T-shirt and black shorts.

I looked up from my seat at the kitchen table, surprised to see him. "I told you on the phone I don't feel like riding," I said glumly.

"I know," he replied. "I wasn't going to come. But then I thought it might be good for you to get out of the house. You know. Get some sunshine. Take your mind off . . . what happened."

He put a hand on my shoulder and kept it there. His hand felt hot through the sleeve of my top.

When he had called at ten to see what time I wanted to go biking, I'd told him about Goggles. "Who would do that?" I had asked, still too upset to even think about it clearly. "Who would be so cruel?"

"It had to be someone at the party," Louis had replied thoughtfully.

Someone at the party.

"I can't go biking today," I'd told him, my voice trembling.

Every time I closed my eyes, I saw Goggles, a bubbling furball, boiled to death in that big pot.

"OK. I understand," Louis replied quietly. "Take it easy, OK?"

But now, three hours later, here he was, standing beside me in the kitchen. I turned and stared up into his startling green eyes. He had a grim, faraway look on his face.

I wondered what he was thinking about.

"It's almost like summer," he said. "It's really great. Come on out. For a short ride. It'll make you feel better. Really."

I turned my gaze to the golden sunlight pouring in through the kitchen window.

"It'll take your mind off Goggles," Louis urged. "Come on. You can't just sit and mope in this kitchen all day. It's too depressing."

"OK," I reluctantly agreed. I scooted the chair back and stood up. Then I called to my mum to tell her I was going out, and followed Louis out the back door.

It was a bright, beautiful day. Everything seemed to shimmer and glow from the sunshine. The grass and trees were that amazing fresh green you only see in springtime.

Two robins were fighting over a long earthworm beside the garage. Our neighbours on both sides were noisily mowing their lawns. I held my ears to block out the roar of the power mowers.

We rode side by side along our usual route. When we got past town, we picked up speed. At first, my legs felt as if they weighed a ton. But as we continued along the road, I started to gain my usual strength.

It took me a while to realize we were headed for the falls.

We left our bikes on the cycle path and walked towards the cliff-edge. The water sparkled pure white as it fell. Above us, the sky was solid blue, not a wisp of a cloud in sight.

Louis walked right up to the edge and peered down. It always made me so nervous when he did that. I stayed several metres back.

After a few seconds, he turned and came over to me. We both sat down on the ground, the falls roaring beneath us.

I decided to tell Louis about how someone was trying to scare me away from him. I'd been thinking about it all night and all morning.

Finally, I'd decided I had to tell him.

He listened to the whole story without moving, a vacant expression on his face. He kept his eyes towards the cliff-edge and didn't react to a thing I said.

"I think the same person killed Goggles," I said, finishing the story, my voice breaking. "But who could it be, Louis? Who?"

He didn't reply.

Turning towards me, he locked his eyes on mine. But he still didn't say anything.

His silence was driving me crazy.

"You *have* to say something!" I demanded. "You can't just stare at me like that after all I've told you."

"I don't know what to say," he said finally, lowering his eyes.

"You know, you can't just be silent all the time," I continued heatedly, "and never tell people what's on your mind. I can tell you're keeping something from me."

He shrugged.

"You've never once mentioned Phoebe," I blurted out.

I think it was the first time I'd mentioned her name in front of him.

"You've never talked about Phoebe once," I continued. "Not once."

He shut his eyes as if trying to shut out my voice.

"I know it's hard for you," I said, softening my tone, seeing the pain on his face. "I know it's hard, but I've got to know, Louis. You've got to tell me the truth."

He opened his eyes. "The truth?"

"You've got to tell me what really happened up here that day."

"Now, wait a minute, Abbie," he started.

I put a hand on his arm. "No. You have to tell me," I insisted. "You have to tell me the whole story about Phoebe. I know you cared about her so much—"

"*Cared* about her?"

His mouth dropped open. He jumped to his feet.

"*Cared* about her?" He stared down at me, his face twisted in excitement. "Are you *crazy*, Abbie? *Cared* about her?" Louis screamed.

"I *hated* Phoebe!" he bellowed. "I hated her so much, I *killed her*!"

# Twenty-One

The roar of the falls grew louder, louder – until I felt as if it were roaring inside my head!

And then I suddenly felt as if my head were about to explode.

"*I hated her so much, I killed her!*"

The words repeated themselves in my mind, over the deafening roar of the sparkling white water beneath us.

Louis stared down at me, his expression wild, his features twisted angrily. His hands were balled into tight fists at his sides as he stood over me. Menacingly.

"*I hated her so much, I killed her!*"

A wave of dread swept over me as I scrambled to my feet.

He had just confessed.

He had just admitted to me that he had killed Phoebe.

And now I was here with him. Alone with him.

The only one to share his terrifying secret.

And he was staring at me with that crazed, dangerous look on his face, staring so intensely into my eyes, as if trying to decide what to do next.

As if trying to decide what to do about me.

As if trying to decide whether or not to push me, too.

"*I hated her so much, I killed her!*"

Why? I wondered.

Why did he do it?

"Louis," I said, taking a step back from the cliff-edge, away from him. "Louis, you . . . pushed Phoebe? Over the falls?" My voice sounded tiny and choked.

I wasn't sure he'd heard me over the relentless roar of the rushing water.

But his expression changed. His forehead wrinkled in consternation. His eyes narrowed. "No," he said. "I didn't push her."

I waited for him to offer more, but he lapsed back into silence.

My entire body shivered. I felt ice-cold despite the bright sunshine. I wrapped my arms round me for warmth, for protection.

But I felt totally alone. Totally vulnerable.

"You said you killed her," I repeated.

He shook his head sadly. "Yes. By bringing her up here. If

I hadn't brought Phoebe here, she wouldn't have died." He let out a groan of pain, of anguish.

"But you didn't push her?" I *had* to know the truth.

He trained his eyes on mine and moved closer to me. "Someone else pushed her," he said. "Someone else."

I stared back at him, searching his eyes, searching his face, trying to tell if what he was telling me was true.

"Someone else," he repeated.

"You mean . . . Courtney?" I asked. "Did Courtney push Phoebe?"

Louis nodded. "Yes."

# Twenty-Two

A flock of birds, tiny dark Vs high in the sky, flew silently overhead, casting no shadow.

Louis took another step towards me.

He was breathing hard. His eyes were narrowed, his jaw clenched tightly.

"Courtney pushed her?" I repeated, not wanting to believe it.

"Yes," he said. "I brought Phoebe up here. But Courtney pushed her."

"*Liar!*"

The voice from the rocks startled us both.

"*Liar! You filthy liar!*"

We both turned to see Courtney running out from behind the tall pile of granite rocks. Her red hair flew wildly about her face, which was twisted in a frightening expression of pure rage.

"Courtney, are you still following me?" Louis cried angrily. "I told you—"

"Shut up!" she shrieked and shoved him hard in the chest, causing him to stumble back a few steps towards the cliff-edge. "Shut up! Shut up! Shut up!"

She tried to push Louis again, but he bumped her away with his shoulder.

Glaring at Louis, Courtney uttered an angry cry.

"I've been covering up for Courtney all this time," Louis said, turning to me.

"Shut up!" Courtney screamed. She turned to me, too. "Don't listen to him. He's a filthy liar!"

"I'm through with lying," Louis said heatedly. "I'm through with covering up for you, Courtney. I can't do it any more."

"Shut up – I'm warning you!" Courtney threatened.

"In January, I wanted to break up with Phoebe," Louis explained, eyeing Courtney warily. "Phoebe and I never got along. We were always fighting. I brought her up here to tell her. Courtney and I brought her here. We were both going to tell Phoebe. Courtney and I had been secretly dating. But, then—"

"Stop it," warned Courtney. "Louis, just shut up. Why are you telling her all this?"

"I started to explain to Phoebe," Louis continued,

ignoring Courtney, staring intently at me, "I started to tell her about Courtney and me. But then Jacob showed up on his bike. I went over there, behind the rocks, to talk to him." He pointed to the rocks.

"And, then," Louis's voice broke as he continued. "And then, while I was talking to Jacob, Courtney pushed Phoebe and her bike over the falls."

Courtney grabbed my arm and swung me around hard. "Don't listen to him, Abbie. It's lies. All lies."

"Courtney – let go of me!" I pleaded, twisting out of her grasp.

"Lies!" Courtney repeated, turning accusingly to Louis. "You've been lying since January. Lying to everyone. Even to yourself."

But Louis continued to ignore her, talking only to me. "After Courtney killed Phoebe, I was ill. I couldn't stand the sight of Courtney. She kept trying to get me to go out with her. But I felt so guilty. So horribly guilty. I didn't want to even *talk* to Courtney again. But she kept following me. She would never leave me alone."

"Liar!"

"Even today!" Louis accused. "Even today you're still following me! Leave me alone, Courtney! Leave me alone!"

Courtney uttered another roar of rage. "Liar!" she cried, giving Louis another shove towards the cliff-edge. "*You* killed

Phoebe! *You* pushed Phoebe! I didn't! *You* were the one! Admit it!"

Courtney turned to me. "Louis, Phoebe and I were up here. We had just started to talk. Then Jacob showed up. Louis went back towards the woods to talk to him. Phoebe and I were standing by the falls. Then I heard someone calling my name. I thought it was Louis. So I left Phoebe and hurried to the woods to find him. When I came back, Louis was standing on the cliff-edge, staring down. And Phoebe was gone. Phoebe was dead."

"Not true!" Louis declared. "I didn't push her – *you* did!"

I cried out as their anger exploded. Louis grabbed Courtney furiously round the waist and wrestled her to the ground.

Shrieking at the top of her lungs, she pounded him with her fists, hitting his face, his chest, his shoulders.

"Stop it! Stop it!" I screamed.

But they didn't hear me.

Locked in a bitter struggle, they wrestled, screaming.

"Stop it – *please!*" I cried.

They were rolling on the ground, rolling towards the cliff-edge.

Courtney was pulling Louis's hair, pummelling his face, batting his chest with her head.

I ran towards them, screaming, begging them to stop.

159

They were only a metre or so from the cliff-edge now.

"Stop it! Stop it, please!" My voice sounded tiny and far away over the roar of the falls.

Courtney scratched her nails down the side of Louis's face. The side of his face turned scarlet, and a line of bright red blood appeared.

He cried out in pain.

"Stop it! *Stop* it!" I didn't recognize my shrill, desperate voice.

Louis grabbed Courtney's head, twisted it round, and pushed her face into the ground.

Her hands thrashed the air wildly as she tried to break out of his hold.

They were only centimetres from the cliff-edge now.

"Stop! Please! Look out!"

They couldn't hear me.

They were out of control, I realized. I was watching the explosion of months of guilt, months of suspicion, months of rage.

Louis and Courtney hated each other because of the secret they shared.

And their hatred was about to kill them both.

"No!" I cried as Courtney rolled away from Louis and, crouched on her knees, pushed him with both hands towards the falls.

I made a lunge for them, reaching to grab Louis's arm and keep him from toppling over the side.

But as I hit the ground, Louis rolled onto his back, reached up, and grabbed Courtney around the knees.

She screamed in protest and broke free.

Then with a breathless snarl of rage, she lunged at him.

He rolled underneath her.

And she plunged over the cliff.

# Twenty-Three

Courtney screamed all the way down.

I didn't hear a splash.

I didn't hear the crack of her body as it slammed onto the jagged black rocks below.

The relentless roar of the falls drowned it out.

The water continued to sparkle and flow. As if it hadn't claimed another victim.

Panting like a wounded animal, Louis raised himself to his knees.

Bright red blood rolled down his cheek.

His eyes were wild, confused.

Still on the ground, I stared at the cliff-edge in disbelief.

Louis was there alone now.

Courtney was gone.

I stared at the spot until my eyes watered over.

I had the urge to run to the edge. To peer down. To see what had happened to poor Courtney.

But I couldn't move. I couldn't breathe.

I had the sudden, crazy thought that if I just stared at the cliff-edge, if I just concentrated hard enough, Courtney would reappear.

I closed my eyes to stop them from watering.

When I opened them, Courtney had not returned.

Only Louis remained, gasping, sucking in deep breaths, his chest heaving under his torn, dirt-stained T-shirt.

It took me a long while to realize that the terrified whimpering sounds I heard were coming from me. My entire body shuddered.

Louis climbed slowly to his feet, still struggling to catch his breath.

I was on my knees, my arms wrapped round my chest.

The roar of the falls grew louder.

Louis stared down at me.

Such an odd expression on his face. Such an odd, hateful expression.

As if he hated me, too.

He took a heavy step towards me, his eyes wild, his jaw clenched tightly.

The blood oozed down the side of his face.

He's a murderer, I realized.

I'm alone now. With a murderer.

He murdered Phoebe. He just murdered Courtney.

And now he's coming to murder me.

*Get up, Abbie*, I told myself, feeling cold panic tighten my throat.

*Get up! Get up!*

Louis slowly moved towards me.

But I couldn't stand up.

# Twenty-Four

"Louis? W-what?" I stammered.

My entire body was trembling.

The falls roared angrily in my ears.

He was a murderer.

He wanted to murder me.

I had to get away.

Uttering a terrified cry, I leaped to my feet. I turned and started to run.

I ran right into Emily.

"Oh!" I cried.

Emily! She was hurrying towards me, running from the cycle path.

"Emily – thank God you're here!" I cried.

I let out a loud sob of relief and threw my arms round her.

"It's OK now," she said softly. "Really, Abbie. It's OK now."

I let her guide me back towards Louis, back towards the cliff-edge.

"But Courtney. . . !" I sobbed. "Courtney fell over the edge! Did you see?"

"I saw it all," Emily said softly, soothingly.

Louis stood at the cliff-edge, hands at his waist. He stared at Emily suspiciously. "What are *you* doing here?" he asked Emily nastily.

"I saw it all," Emily told him. "I was back at the rocks, and I saw everything that happened."

"You mean. . ." Louis started.

"I saw Abbie push Courtney over the cliff," Emily said.

"Huh?" I cried out in confusion. *What* had Emily just said?

I pulled away from her, but she blocked my path. She took a step forward, her eyes narrowing.

I had no choice. I took a step back, towards the falls.

"I saw Abbie push Courtney over the cliff," Emily told Louis.

"No!" I shrieked.

"Then," Emily continued calmly, ignoring me, speaking only to Louis, "Abbie tried to push *you* over the side. But Abbie slipped, and she accidentally fell herself."

An odd smile formed on Emily's face. "Isn't that a shame?" she asked Louis sarcastically. "Poor Abbie."

# Twenty-Five

Listening to Emily and her deliberate lies made something inside me snap.

My terror disappeared, replaced by anger.

I felt the red current of anger I had felt that afternoon in the gym.

"Why are you *doing* this?" I demanded of her. "Why are you saying all this? You *know* it isn't true!"

Emily laughed. "But it *is* true. Isn't it, Louis?" She turned back to me, tossing her dishevelled black hair behind her shoulder. "At least, that's what Louis and I will tell everyone after you're gone, Abbie."

Louis rubbed his cheek where the blood had turned dark and was starting to cake. "I don't get it, Emily," he said quietly.

Emily uttered a moan of frustration. "No, Louis. I guess you *don't!*" she exclaimed bitterly. "Well, let me explain it to

167

you. Why do you think I've put up with that idiot Jacob all these months?"

Louis didn't answer. He stared back at her, rubbing his wounded face.

"I couldn't stand Jacob," Emily said angrily, practically spitting the words. "But I stayed with him just to be close to you." She took a deep breath. "After I killed Phoebe, I thought that you and I. . ."

Louis and I both let out loud cries of surprise.

"*You* killed Phoebe?" Louis asked, his face bright red, his eyes revealing deep pain along with his surprise.

Emily laughed bitterly. "All these months, you and Courtney suspected each other. What a riot. I enjoyed that. I really did."

"But, Emily—" Louis started.

Emily cut him off. "I thought it would be you and me after that, Louis. But you didn't know I was alive. Even after I killed for you. First, Courtney wouldn't let you alone. Then. . ." Emily raised her eyes to me, her features twisted in hatred.

"Then, Abbie came along. With her perfect blonde hair and her perfect little figure. I tried to scare Abbie away. I really tried. But. . ."

It had been Emily all along, I realized. Emily, who slashed my bike tyres, who rigged the computer, who made those threatening calls, who murdered Goggles.

Crazy Emily.

My friend.

My friend, who was crazy enough about Louis to kill for him.

And kill again.

"Enough talk," she said in a low whisper. "Louis, say goodbye to Abbie."

I stiffened my muscles, readied myself, prepared to duck away from her and run.

But she was faster than I'd imagined.

Before I could react, she lunged forward.

She ran into me, lowering her shoulder like a football lineman, backing me to the edge.

And before I could even cry out in horror, I went sailing over the falls.

# Twenty-Six

I mean, in that blind second of heart-stopping panic, I *imagined* myself toppling over the falls.

I cried out and sank to my knees on the edge as I realized that Emily had failed. As I realized that I was safe.

The water rushed loudly below me.

My heart pounded even louder.

I was safe. Safe on the ground. Safe on hard, solid ground.

I raised my eyes to see Louis with his arms round Emily's legs. He had tackled her from behind.

And now he was holding her face down on the ground, pinning her there with both hands as she thrashed and squirmed and tried to free herself.

A blue light started flashing in the sky.

Was I going crazy?

No.

I pulled myself to my feet, blinking against the flashing blue light.

The flashing blue light of a police car.

Two uniformed policemen were hurrying towards us.

"Throw me over!" Emily screamed to Louis, struggling desperately to get out from under him. "Throw me over, too! I know you want to! I know you hate me enough!"

But Louis kept her pinned to the ground until one of the policemen pulled him away and grabbed Emily's arms.

"H-how did you get here?" I stammered to his partner. "I mean, how did you know we were here?"

"Your friend," he answered flatly, his face completely expressionless.

"Friend?" I stared at him in total bewilderment.

He pointed down over the falls.

I took a step towards the edge and looked down. An ambulance stood on the near bank of the river.

"She was lucky," the policeman said in the same monotone.

"Courtney?" I cried, staring wide-eyed as two paramedics helped someone into the back of the ambulance.

"Yeah. She's got a broken arm. Some broken ribs. But she walked out. She told us you were up here. Good thing, huh?"

I uttered a sigh of relief. Courtney was going to be OK.

When I turned back, both policemen were leading Emily to their car. She was still struggling. Still screaming hysterically, "Throw me over! Throw me over, too!"

Louis made his way to me and put his arm round my shoulder.

"Do you two need a ride home?" one of the policemen called, holding the driver's door open.

"No. We can ride our bikes," Louis answered.

"Get cleaned up. Then come to the station. We'll need statements from you both," the policeman instructed. He slid behind the wheel and slammed the door hard.

His partner was in the back seat with Emily, who was still screaming and crying.

A few seconds later, the police car squealed away.

Louis took my hand and led me back to our bikes. He sighed wearily. "Who says nothing ever happens in small towns?"

I shook my head. "I think it's going to get a lot more boring from now on," I replied.

"Hope so," he said quietly.

Then he let his bike fall to the ground as he put his arms round me, pulled me close, and kissed me.

He was sweaty and smelly. He was covered in dirt, and his face was caked with dried blood.

I kissed him back.

I hardly even noticed.